DINNER AFTER DEATH

11/12 pt Baskerville. Linotype
21 X 35 lines + headline + folio
Crown 8vo.

DINNER AFTER DEATH

Maintaining law and order in Avigron was little more than a routine task for stolid, methodical, conscientious Inspector Angriz, head of the local gendarmerie, that is, until two women are brutally murdered in almost identical circumstances.

Baffled by these circumstances and the time lag, he decided to seek assistance from the Sûreté, only to be told by Inspector Lotti, France's most implacable investigator, that he has not *one* but *two* problems on his hands. A third murder, that of the lovely Lucille Evremont, complicates matters further.

How these problems are eventually resolved is the gripping "no holds barred" story of *Dinner After Death*.

DINNER
AFTER
DEATH

T. IRVING-JAMES

ROBERT HALE LIMITED
63 Old Brompton Road, London S.W.7

TO MY WIFE

None of the characters in this book is a portrait of a living person nor did the incidents here recorded ever take place.

*Printed in Great Britain by
East Midland Printing Co. Ltd.
Bury St. Edmunds, Suffolk*

CHAPTER I

PIERRE MOLAY regarded Inspector Lotti with a disdainful expression.

"So. . . ." He shrugged his large shoulders, "they have sent you all the way from Paris just to see me?"

Inspector Lotti shook his head.

"You flatter yourself, *Monsieur*. Nobody *sent* me."

"But you are from the—?"

"Yes, yes, from the Sûreté!" Molay's overbearing confidence and thinly veiled contempt were already beginning to annoy the Inspector. "But as I am here to enquire into the murder of Lucille Evremont, I may speak to every man and woman in Avigron."

"All thirty thousand of them? And what about the children?" The mockery was reflected in the dark penetrating eyes. "Then you will be very busy for many weeks to come, Inspector."

"It may take a long time, but justice has plenty of time."

"Ah, a terrible thing!"

Molay was laughing inwardly. He was not at all disturbed by the presence of Inspector Lotti and his assistant, Sergeant Tulle. He had nothing to fear.

Lucille had been a lovely girl. Astonishingly beautiful. A stranger to the town, her body had been dragged from the bed of the river by the police. She had been strangled.

This was the third killing in the area. On the face of it, the same motive had prompted the same person to murder. All the victims had been women. All had died in the same way.

Baffled by the previous crimes, and fearing that others might soon follow, the local police, led by Inspector Angriz, had asked for assistance. In response to the request, this poker-faced, chill-eyed sleuth had come from Paris to enquire into the death of Lucille Evremont. He was regarded as the most able man at the Sûreté. At least three killers had gone to the guillotine because of his patience, determination and refusal to admit he was beaten.

Molay was in no way awed by his visitor. He was afraid of no man. During the Occupation, he had gone in danger of his life for close on three years. He had deceived the Germans. With equal cunning and success, he had misled the French Resistance.

He was a man who compelled attention, even in a crowd. He was fully six feet three inches in his bare feet, and his build in every way complemented his size. Wide, muscular shoulders, powerful arms, ham-like hands, exceptionally hairy chest, and legs that were strong and fleet.

His face was square, and crowned with a mass of black curls, which were always in disarray and rarely combed. The forehead low and heavy-browed, the eyes cautious and suspicious. The nose large, but not too much so for such a face, and the mouth was sensuous and had a looseness that indicated cruelty.

"You knew Lucille Evremont, *Monsieur*?"

"I did."

"She visited you here?"

"Ah!" Molay spoke with an exasperating slowness. "The clever inspector is trying to trap Molay. He knows she came here."

"I am not trying to trap you." Lotti knew Molay was being deliberately provocative, but he found it hard to keep his patience. "I wish only to discover the truth."

"The truth! Yes! But where does one even start to look for truth in Avigron?" There was no hint of a smile on the large face. The look was one of naked insolence.

"We can start here. How often did Lucille Evremont visit you?"

"Does the clever inspector already know the answer to that one, as well?"

"I am asking you."

"Once. She came here just once. A memorable visit!"

"Memorable?"

"She was so good to see. Her breasts! They were *magnifique*! So full—so rounded—so firm! And her legs! Ah, they were more entrancing than all the seven Pillars of Wisdom!"

"I have seen them, *Monsieur*. She was, indeed, incomparable."

"So you noticed! Ah, what madman was it who would destroy so much beauty? I trust, Inspector, you arrange an early appointment for him with Madame Guillotine."

"I shall certainly do my best. But I must ask you, *Monsieur*, where were you on the evening of May the ninth?"

Molay gazed reflectively at a point some twelve inches above the inspector's head.

"Now where. . . .? The ninth? What day was that?"

"Tuesday."

"Ah, yes, Tuesday. Now I know where I was."

"Where?"

"Here, Inspector."

Lotti was finding it hard to resist his desire to storm into Molay. But Inspector Angriz had already warned him of the man's arrogance. It would serve no purpose to let Molay see that he was being as disturbing as he intended to be.

The Inspector ran a cursory eye over the workshop. It contained a couple of rough-hewn work benches. On a dais, covered by a tricolour, in front of the window were displayed one new and four or five second-hand bicycles.

"What do you do, *Monsieur*?"

"The inspector has eyes." Molay pointed indifferently to the benches on which were several tools and a motley assortment of bicycle parts—frames, chains, brakes, cables and tyres.

"You sell and repair bicycles, it seems?"

"I do. But, alas, trade is poor these days. The motor-car has quite ruined my business. For a time, just after the war, trade was good. But, of late, as the clever inspector will know, bicycles have become much less fashionable as a means of transportation. Pedalling, it is considered bad for the heart."

Lotti was eyeing him narrowly.

"You have little to do these days?"

"Far too little."

"Then what were you doing here on the evening of May the ninth?"

Molay laughed scornfully.

"So the cunning inspector *was* laying a trap! He thought he would catch the ignorant Molay unawares and stampede him into saying something that would incriminate him! Inspector, that is very naughty of you!"

The colour rushed to Inspector Lotti's face. As one of France's leading criminal investigators, he was accustomed to at least a show of respect. Never had he encountered such conceit in any man.

"You have not answered my question, Molay."

"So the inspector is not satisfied?"

"Be so kind as to answer."

"Now, what was I doing?" The sly look had returned to Molay's eyes. "I might have been making love to my wife. A most pleasant pastime—if I had a wife. But, alas, I can afford no such luxury. Molay must be content with his cold and lonely bed."

"Will you tell me—?"

"But, of course, Inspector." Molay had been playing for time. His position was not as sound as it might have been. He had good reason to send the police away in a satisfied frame of mind. Not that he had murdered Lucille Evremont, although, by God. . . . He turned his attention again to the problem.

"Well?" snapped Lotti.

"I was entertaining my friend—my very dear friend —Jean Gavroche."

"All evening?"

"All the evening. It is not often he comes here, you understand."

"But if he is your friend. . . ?"

"Ah, it is his wife, you see, Inspector. She is a terrible woman. A tyrant. Makes Jean's life miserable. Commands him like a captain in the Foreign Legion. And never, never allows him the consolation of her body. Not even on Bastille Day. Can you imagine that? His wife, and she will not even permit him to share her bed!"

"It is not a unique situation," said Lotti dryly. "Where does Jean Gavroche live?"

"Just round the corner. But beware of his wife. She is a witch. And what a tongue! A sword dipped in acid."

"Come!" Lotti turned to his sergeant. "We are wasting our time here—at the moment."

"Ah! Then I can look forward to the pleasure of a further visit from the famous Inspector?"

"Perhaps." The Inspector moved to the door. "But if there is any pleasure in our visit, believe me, it will be all yours."

And before Molay could think of a suitable reply, they had gone. He went to the window and watched them climb into their car. He resented the intrusion. No man, he felt, had a right to question him. Nevertheless, he knew he must not excite their suspicion. Once they got the idea that he was connected with the death of Lucille Evremont, they would never leave him alone. Night and day, they would be watching him and his premises. And that would be awkward—very awkward indeed.

He saw the police car out of sight, then went into the room at the back of his shop. It was sparsely furnished despite the fact that it was an all-purpose room. There was a bed in one corner—unmade. There was a table in another corner, still littered with the crockery and cutlery he had used for his breakfast and midday meal. There were a couple of nondescript dining chairs and one deep easy chair. The carpets were worn, in places threadbare, and the curtains had obviously not been washed for a long time.

It was the room of a bachelor, and of a bachelor who was content to satisfy his physical needs of eating and sleeping in surroundings not far removed from those of a pig-sty.

Molay crossed to a cupboard, tugged open the protesting door, and from it extracted a pot-bellied bottle of wine. He filled a large glass and began to drink. He sipped the wine slowly, savouring to the full each separate mouthful. That was typical of him. He enjoyed all the material pleasures, taking his time over them, extracting the greatest possible delight from every second. And if anyone hindered or tried to interfere with him, that was a most serious matter. At times, deadly serious.

The bell rang as someone opened the street door into the shop.

"Pierre! Are you there?"

"Is that you, Gavroche?"

The inner doorway darkened as a figure occupied it. The man was small and had an uncertain air. His eyes were nervously restless, as if he was always in a state of anxious watchfulness.

"So it is you." Molay's tone lacked enthusiasm.

"I see you had the police enquiring about Lucille Evremont, eh?" The rounded, pasty cheeks shook.

"So that's why you came!" Molay's voice was sour. "To make sure your wretched little hide was safe?"

"Oh, no, Pierre." Gavroche stepped into the room and removed his cap. He revealed a head that was completely bald. "What did you tell them?"

Molay laughed, and it was a cruel sound. "I referred them to you."

Gavroche uttered a squeal of alarm. "To-to me!"

"Yes, Jean." Molay took another sip of wine and

held it in his mouth for a few moments. Only after he had swallowed did he say: "Of course, I did not tell them that you murdered Lucille Evremont."

"M-me! M-murder—"

"In fact, I made you quite safe. I told them you were here, my friend."

"H-here? When?"

"On the evening of the murder."

"Oh!" Gavroche ran a shaking hand over his skull. "B-but I wasn't here, Pierre."

"Do you think I didn't know that?"

"Then why—"

"I needed an alibi. Someone to tell the police that *I* was here because they were here with me." Molay's mouth twisted with malicious pleasure. "Who better could I say than my dear friend, Jean Gavroche? Who would be more willing to testify for me?"

Gavroche tried to speak, but no words came. He was appalled. He had always dreaded the police. Besides, if his wife were to learn—

Molay's fist crashing on to the table startled him greatly.

"You remember, Gavroche?" There was naked menace in the voice. "You talked to me *all* evening. Remember?"

"Y-yes, b-but—"

"Of course. You spent most of your time complaining about your wife. You said how very cold she was."

"Yes, I did, Pierre. I remember now."

"I should just think you do! And what was it you said about how happy you would be with a new, young wife?"

Gavroche knew that all this play-acting had a serious purpose. It was designed to give protection to Molay.

It might involve him in some very awkward—even impossible—questions, but Molay cared nothing for that. He was concerned only to take care of himself. If Gavroche suffered as a consequence, then that was just too bad for Gavroche.

"Well, Jean, what did you say about a fresh, young wife?"

"That—that she'd be very nice, Pierre."

Molay slapped his thigh. He was greatly amused. The little man's nervousness and timid statement pleased him.

"Is that all it would be? Why, man, it would mean a new life for you. You'd shed your years as a tree sheds leaves."

"Y-yes, Pierre, I suppose I would."

The truth was, and Molay suspected it, that Gavroche had always been an inept lover and his wife had decided on permanent nocturnal separation from him because, in her despair, she could do no other.

"Very well, Jean. If the police ask you where you were on the night of May the ninth, you have an alibi in me. You say you were here."

"B-but the police don't suspect that I—?"

"They suspect every man in Avigron."

"Not me, though. I wouldn't kill anyone, least of all a good-looking girl like Lucille Evremont."

"Ah, I know you wouldn't." Molay poured himself another glass of wine, but he did not offer his visitor a drink. "But the police don't know that. Don't you see what a perilous position you are in?"

Gavroche's eyes blinked wide open.

"M-m-me? W-w-why?"

"Isn't it obvious? You are known to live a celibate life, even though you are married. What does that do

to a man over the years? Drives him to desperation.
Makes him lose his head, so that he attacks and rapes
an innocent girl—sometimes without knowing."

"No! no!" The cry was a pitiful bleat.

"Of course not—not normally." Molay delighted
in tormenting the hapless Gavroche. "But that Inspector Lotti's cunning—very cunning. There isn't a secret
in Avigron he won't have unearthed before the month
is out. He'll know all about you and that iceberg of a
wife of yours. And he'll know just what to think about
it."

"But he can't imagine that I—"

"Not if you tell him you were here all the evening
of May the ninth talking to me. Depend on it, *mon
ami*, I'll tell him the same thing. For your sake as well
as mine."

"And I shall be all right, Pierre?"

"Haven't I told you so already? You'll be quite all
right."

"Y-yes, of course. But the heroin? What about
that?"

Molay's expression changed.

"You haven't received the latest delivery yet?" He
spoke sharply, almost threateningly.

"No, Pierre."

"When is it due?"

"Tonight. It will be brought up river in the usual
way."

"Then we cannot stop it. It is too late for that."

"Pierre!" Gavroche was shaking visibly. His mouth
was a tremble. "What are we to do?"

"There is nothing we can do. You must bring it
here as already arranged. In any case, there is little
risk that the *gendarmes* will find it. It is a murderer

they are seeking. Not heroin. And it is well hidden.
They have not guessed all this time. Why should they
guess now, when they are thinking of other things?"

Gavroche was by no means reassured. He had spent
a thoroughly wretched day, knowing that there was
so much police activity in the town. Gavroche was
afraid of almost everything and everybody. Of his
wife. Of the police. Of Molay. It was Molay who had
frightened him into acting as agent for that heroin all
those months ago. Since then, he had spent many sleep-
less nights and many anxious moments. Although all
he did was carry the stuff from the river to Molay's
premises.

The route was not long, and there was nothing
whatever to arouse suspicion. The contact placed the
stuff in Gavroche's jacket lining and pockets, or in the
saddlebag of the cycle on which he rode to and from
his job. The machine provided him with an excellent
cover for his irregular visits to Molay's workshop.

Gavroche was paid but poorly for his services, and
he would have been greatly relieved to have done with
the whole alarming business. He had hinted as much
to Molay more than once.

"Oh, no!" Molay had retorted on each occasion.
"You're in this, and in it you'll stay. You're well-paid
for the little you do. And you're not going to run out
on me like this. If you so much as try. . . ."

Molay never completed his threat in words, but the
huge fists he brought up to within inches of Gavroche's
face were more than enough.

It was very much in Molay's interests that Gavroche
should continue to receive the heroin on its arrival at
Avigron. He worked on the river, giving directions to
the barges that kept it clear of mud. His presence in

the vicinity of the river excited no curiosity. He could go there whenever he wished, day or night, in perfect safety.

The *gendarmerie* had known for some time that heroin was passing through the town, but they had so far failed to detect how it came in and went out again. And it was Gavroche's part in its transit which went far to explain why the police had not succeeded in intercepting it. He was such an innocent façade, so nervous and insignificant, they had never troubled to investigate him.

Suspicious of Molay, they had made a search of his premises more than once, without finding anything. Yet it was from his workshop that the heroin went out to several of France's largest cities.

Molay was without fear. It was, perhaps, his one real virtue. Certainly, it was his strength and security. He was so contemptuous of the police, and he mocked them so scathingly, they betrayed a certain uneasiness in his presence. His vast confidence seemed to unnerve them.

Gavroche was eyeing him most miserably.

"B-but if the *gendarmes* see me and decide to search me—?"

"That's a risk you'll have to take," Molay interrupted impatiently. "*Mon Dieu*, man, life's all chance. So stop shivering and make up your mind you'll do as I say."

"Oh dear, oh dear!" Gavroche was wringing his hands in his anguish. "Listen, *mon ami*, you visit the boat and collect the—"

He stopped speaking abruptly. Molay had jerked to his feet, his fists raised menacingly.

"Listen to me, Gavroche! You'll do as I say or. . . ."

He moved towards Gavroche, eyes smouldering, flexing his fingers. Even before he had the little man by the shoulders, Gavroche had capitulated.

"Yes, yes, Pierre, I'll do it," he babbled. "I'll do it —gladly!"

Molay pushed him away, causing him to stagger back and crash into the side of the door.

"See that you do! And now, away with you! And, for pity's sake, try not to look so frightened and guilty. If you don't take care, they'll haul you in suspected of killing Lucille because you look as if you did."

He watched Gavroche go. The thin shoulders were stooped, the head hung dejectedly. He followed him with contemptuous eyes. He saw most men as he saw Gavroche—spineless. They deserved to be used and exploited. They were obviously made to do the bidding of strong men like himself. Bah, they were unworthy of his consideration.

He remained looking out into the street. It was spring, and the evening air was still warm.

So Lucille Evremont was dead. Would he have to make do with Cosette again? He had had her, naked and adoring. She was submissive, the way he liked them. But she was insipid. Indeed, compared with Lucille Evremont, she was nothing at all. Lucille! Ah, what a woman she had been! Almost he. . . . .

But the thought that he had missed so much was unbearable. He turned back to the bottle and poured himself a generous libation of wine.

CHAPTER II

IN 1942, WHEN France was beginning her third year of anguish under the German occupation, Pierre Molay was twenty. It was a dangerous world in which he found himself. But danger exhilarated him. Even when he had experienced all the excitements of love, this sensation, he felt, matched them.

Already, he possessed the aplomb necessary to ensure his safety under difficult and precipitous circumstances. His natural cunning told him that all the advantages he needed were to be gained by playing one side off against the other. This made all contacts possible, and provided ample cover for his many dubious activities. Not the least of these was an intimate knowledge of Black Market requirements, as well as the means to buy from it whatever he wanted.

He knew he was dicing with death, but he experienced no fear on that account. He took the view that those who obeyed the rules were no safer than he who was breaking them. Men, women, and even children, were spirited away during the night, or called for interrogation, and were never seen again. Germans and their agents, as well as members of their Fifth Column, also vanished, nothing more being heard of them.

Despite his shrewdness and the immense care with which he worked, the day came when he realised he had lost the confidence of the local Gestapo Headquarter's staff. He knew he was in great peril. He was aware that, for him, imprisonment in a concentration camp would be brief but terrible. There would be no mercy for a man who had double-crossed the Wehrmacht.

His subtle brain suggested a way of rehabilitating himself in their estimation. On the pretext that he was taking him to see a British agent, who had been parachuted into the district, he persuaded a leading member of the Resistance to accompany him to a rendezvous where the Germans were waiting to seize him.

He saw the look of hatred and contempt which flashed in the eyes of the betrayed man as the ambush closed in on him, but it gave him no cause for concern. He knew quite well the sort of treatment that would be meted out to his fellow Frenchman, but he felt no compunction. His world was governed by the law of kill, or be killed, and Molay had a passionate desire to live.

His act of treachery achieved its purpose. The Gestapo were now firmly convinced that he was, indeed, devoted to their cause. But he could not allow things to remain there. He had to restore the faith of the Resistance, otherwise he would end up in some dark alley, a knife in his back.

Obedient to the one tenet of his jungle creed that he must kill, or be killed, he lured a German agent into an empty cellar and there stabbed him to death before he had a chance to realise his danger. Then he invited three lieutenants of the local Maquis to view the body. Any doubts they had were dispersed. He was once again accepted as a trustworthy comrade in the fight for freedom.

The killing revealed to him the pleasure—amounting to an ecstasy—such an act inspired. He now felt that the taking of life was even more enjoyable than the act of creating it. There had been an intense thrill, affecting all the nerves in his stomach, as he saw the look of appalled astonishment in the eyes of his victim as the thrusting knife pierced his heart.

His experience was to be repeated several times with Germans before they were finally driven out. But he was disappointed to find that the expected excitement did not materialise when he despatched them with a pistol fitted with a silencer. It was then that he realised that the delight in killing could only come if he had actual physical contact with the one he had been detailed to destroy.

It was for that reason he undertook a killing of his own. It served a double purpose. It was obvious that the tide of war was running against the Third Reich. Hitler's hold on Europe was being steadily loosened. The day when they withdrew from France could not be far distant. It was essential to prove beyond all doubt where his sympathies lay. He guessed that many things would come to light once the occupation forces had left. There would be questions, there might even be French men and women who knew things they were keeping secret against the day of reckoning.

Such a day, he knew, was bound to dawn. The Resistance had lists of those who had collaborated with the enemy. They were not being kept for nothing. When the last jackboot had gone, the vengeance would come, and it would be swift and very terrible. Molay was determined to be above suspicion.

Like all Frenchmen, Molay had often marvelled at the lack of imagination shown by the Germans. It was amazingly easy to deceive them, although difficult indeed to escape once they got on a man's trail.

To the second-in-command of the local Gestapo he produced a crude sketch provided by the Resistance. It purported to show a house in which the underground had their Headquarters.

The German had risen to the bait and had eagerly consented to accompany him. He had suddenly seized his unsuspecting companion by the throat and strangled him. Seeing the bulging, terrified eyes, the sagging jaw, and feeling the hands feebly clawing at his chest, the killing had been so mentally stimulating, it was almost a pain.

Molay saw the invaders of his native soil scurry back across their own frontiers with no little regret. Once the long-harboured hates against traitors and Fifth Columnists had been satisfied, the State quickly reasserted its authority. Murder was again a crime in law, and anyone found guilty of it was only too likely to keep a single disagreeable tryst with Madame Guillotine. He felt cheated.

He comforted himself with the thought that there was love. At least, the kind of love which he understood and which he so revelled in.

"A world without women," he confided to Gavroche. "Ah, what an impossible place it would be! How dull and dreary!"

Gavroche, united to a woman who despised him, was not convinced.

"A world without women would be marvellous, Pierre. Paradise would always have been paradise had there been no Eve. Take my wife—"

"God forbid!" Molay interrupted cruelly.

"If only He had forbidden me! Look at her! She takes every centime I earn."

"More fool you for giving it to her!"

"But I am helpless. If I do not meet all her demands, she threatens to turn me out. If she knew about . . . the . . . the other money, she would inform on me to the police."

Molay scowled at that.

"Go to the *gendarmerie*, indeed! If ever she *does* find out, tell her to go ahead. She would merely be cutting off that sharp nose of hers to spite her face. She's too clever to do any such thing."

"I dare not take the chance! I dare not! *Mon Dieu!* The penalties for smuggling are terrible—simply terrible!"

"Then tell her that, if she so much as whispers a word about our activities, she will have to reckon with me. Tell her, *mon ami*, that I would wring her scraggy neck. Yes, and tell her I mean it."

But Gavroche was too afraid of his wife to try to intimidate her with threats. He ignored the remark and continued plaintively:

"What do I get for my money?" his chin quivering. "Nothing! Nothing except indigestion. That woman's cooking! You'd never believe it. She burns everything —everything!"

"But doesn't even warm you."

"But what can I do about that? She refuses to share my bed. How can I make her accept me? There was the warmth in her—once. Too much warmth, really. Do you know, Pierre, she would waken me in the middle of the night. Yes, in the middle of the night, when I was already quite spent and desperately needing sleep. 'Jean,' she would say, 'I need you again. Come, take me!' What self-respecting woman speaks to her husband in such a way."

Delighted by Gavroche's scandalized expression, Molay rocked with laughter.

"Lots . . . I . . . imagine. After all, a husband has duties. A wife has the right to expect he will fulfil them."

"But there are limits."

"Some women don't think so." He wagged an admonitory finger at Gavroche. "It seems you were not an adequate husband, *mon ami*. No woman will forgive that. It is felt as an insult. After all, a husband should be attracted by his wife—at least, sufficient to meet her needs. When he isn't, then—pouf!—her heart grows cold. And she begins to seek solace elsewhere."

It was a sly jibe, being common knowledge that his wife had had two or three lovers.

"You should have known better than to marry."

"But I wanted Marie. I loved her. I was mad for her."

"And now you're mad because you've got her."

"But her mother never left us. What else could I do but marry her?"

"Do! You might have tried marrying the mother. You should have recognised the set-up for what it was —a trap, and kept your freedom. Like I have kept mine. Then you could have had whatever woman you fancied—and on *your* terms."

There was no kindness in the advice. Anyone less appealing to women than Gavroche, it was hard to imagine. *A wizened edition of a baby*, was how Molay thought of him.

His own case was quite different. His size and strength, as well as his ruthlessness, had always drawn their attention.

He had his first experience of the opposite sex when
he was only twelve. By then, physically, he was virtually a man, being head and shoulders taller than the
other children of his age. His voice was fast deepening,
and there was a shadow on his chin, the beginnings of
a beard. Mentally, however, he was still a boy. His
attitude to the female was one of disdain or indifference. To his school-fellows, who spent much of their
time looking covertly at the swelling outlines of
blouses, he would say: "Girls! Bah! What does a boy
want with them."

It was Madame Brujon who gave him the answer.
A relief teacher, she travelled around the primary
schools in the area taking classes in English and arith-
metic. She was, Molay judged, about forty, a great age
to him at that time. But she was pleasant. She had dark
hair she arranged well, having it frame her sweet face
like a rain cloud. She had, too, a mouth shaped like
a bow, and eyes that were sombre and shadowed with
a lingering discontent. Her figure commanded little
attention. Those who knew her described it as rather
plump, but quite passable. She was, in fact, deep-
chested, wide-hipped, and not much more than
slender.

Her husband had been killed in a road accident
some seven years after their marriage, and necessity
had compelled her to return to the profession, though
she seemed able to manage by working part-time.

During lessons he often found her gaze fixed on him,
as if she were trying to estimate just what kind of boy
he was. He found her interest embarrassing, fearing
the other boys might notice. If they did, they would
bait him mercilessly.

Then, one never-to-be-forgotten afternoon, Madame Brujon said to him:

"Pierre, I wish you to stay behind after school. It seems you do not really understand fractions."

He felt rebellious. He was not interested in the subject and lacked the will to concentrate. His size led him to feel that lessons were beneath him. He *was* a man really, and considered he ought to have been engaged in grown-up pursuits.

He stayed behind after the rest had gone, but his face betrayed his resentment.

Madame Brujon was smiling at him, and it wasn't like any he had seen on her face before.

"Stay where you are, Pierre. I will come to you."

Carrying his exercise book, she left her desk, her eyes embracing him. He had never felt so uncomfortable. At the same time he experienced strange stirrings within him, and a tension that was altogether to his liking.

When she reached him, he became aware of a scent he had never noticed about her before. It brought a warmth to his skin as he inhaled it.

"You're a strange boy, Pierre," she said, still smiling. "But I like you."

She bent to place his book on the low desk. Her action drew his gaze. He felt the colour mount in his face. Her blouse was unbuttoned almost halfway down. In this position, the edges had fallen wide apart and he could see her breasts—all of them. He could not look away. They were full and so seductively curved, with proud coronets, pink and most beautifully circled. He longed to reach out and touch them.

Her stillness told him she knew where his eyes

rested. With a shock of amazement he realised she had meant him to see them.

"Pierre. I wonder. . . ."

"Yes?"

"Are you man enough to keep secrets? I mean big and very important secrets."

"If you don't think I am—" He resented her questioning.

She showed no surprise at his attitude.

"Pierre, I want you to come to my home tonight."

"What for?"

"I wish to show you things that will interest you. Things you must never speak about to a living soul. Never! Never! Never!"

He hesitated.

"You won't be sorry," she urged.

"What will it be worth to me?" he demanded roughly.

"Worth?" She thought for some moments. "Ten francs."

"Ten!" He was surprised. "Very well, I will come."

"Good." She straightened and looked at him, her face wearing a most solemn expression. "You will tell no one you are coming?"

"No one."

"And, afterwards, no one that you have been?"

"Haven't I already said?"

"Yes, yes."

"If you can't trust me—"

"I can! Of course I can!" She was standing very close to him. "Shall we say seven o'clock, then? Come to the back door, and don't let anyone see you."

He nodded absently, his eyes on the generous curves of her hips.

"What will you tell your mother?"

"Nothing, except that I'm going out."

"Will she be satisfied with that?"

"She'll have to be."

"I see." She bent once more. Again the edges of her blouse fell outwards.

He sensed there was something significant in this gesture, and that it promised a quite tremendous experience.

CHAPTER III

AT HOME, having his tea, Pierre felt a curious excitement. It interfered with the swallowing of his food. It kept a colour in his cheeks. He was not given to talk for its own sake, but he was more than usually quiet at the table.

His mother, who had long since ceased to exercise any parental authority, kept eyeing him intently. Truth to tell, she was awed by the realisation that this was her son. She was below average height, and his father had displayed no outstanding physical qualities.

At last, mustering enough courage, she said: "Pierre, are you all right?"

"I'm all right."

Used to his manner, she was not surprised by the surly nature of the reply. Inclined to be taciturn herself, she disliked any show of emotion as much as he did. This made intimate exchanges between them impossible.

Impatiently he pushed his plate away and made for the sink in the kitchen. There, stripped to the waist, he washed with a care he had never exercised before. His hair, always a problem because it tangled so readily, he struggled with in vain for several minutes.

He wore his usual clothes, but he put his jacket on with greater care, brushing it down thoroughly. He even cleaned his shoes—a rare occurrence.

Going up to his room, he eyed himself critically in the mirror. He felt he should look his best.

At six-fifteen he was ready to go, but darkness had not yet fallen and it was much too early.

He remained in his room, restlessly walking the floor, pausing now and then to regard his reflection. Finally, unable to contain his impatience any longer, he went downstairs.

Already mystified by his behaviour, his mother stared in open amazement at his clean appearance.

"Going out, Pierre?"

"I am."

"Where?"

He ignored the question, and she knew him well enough to be sure that nothing would persuade him to tell her, but she decided to venture one more feeler.

"Will you be away long?"

"Perhaps."

"Don't you know?"

He did not answer. Instead, he went out. There was a troubled expression on her face as he slammed the door.

Twilight was deepening to darkness as he stepped into the street. The home of Madame Brujon was on the outskirts of the town, about twenty minutes walk away. Standing behind its own little apron of lawn in a narrow surround of garden, there were houses to the left and right, but there was no actual contact. The isolation, more illusory than real, gave a reassuring sense of privacy.

Though he knew he was early, Pierre could not help hurrying. At a quarter to seven he was opening the rear gate.

He went boldly to the door and knocked. It was opened almost at once. Madame Brujon's face lit up at the sight of him.

"Come in, Pierre." She spoke softly as if afraid of being overheard. The moment he was over the threshold she closed and bolted the door. Her manner was one of conspiracy which served to excite him.

Leading the way to a small, cosy sitting-room, in the centre of which was a divan suggestively set with cushions, she invited him to sit down.

By the glow of an electric fire and two small-powered wall lights, he could see that the prevailing decor was pink, while the curtains drawn across the window were a deep red. It was a colour he found disconcerting.

"Would you like some wine, Pierre?"

"Yes, *Mademoiselle*."

"Not *Mademoiselle*, please. Not here. I'm sure you can say Annette."

Producing a bottle of wine and two glasses from a cabinet in the corner, she poured generously for both of them, then sat down beside him eyes shining with warm anticipation. He had never seen her look so happy.

"Like it?"

"Yes. It tastes so good I'm making it last."

"Empty your glass. There's lots more if you want it."

He drank it then. Within minutes he had downed half the replenishment. His world was now rosier than he had ever known it. A world of incredible sensations quite detached from reality.

"How do you feel now, Pierre?"

"I don't know."

"Aren't you pleased to be here with me?" She was suddenly concerned.

"More than that."

Putting down her glass she slipped her arm about his shoulders with an assumed carelessness, but tightened her grip when he did not object. With her wine-laden breath sweet in his nostrils, she took his hand and slid it beneath her blouse. He acted instinctively and buried his head against her bare bosom.

Helped by Annette, he pursued his aim. He heard her whimpering, moaning, sobbing beneath him. Then she uttered a cry—a curious mixture of triumph, submission and pure delight.

As for Pierre, he experienced a savage, pleasurable pain that was almost unbearable.

When she withdrew from him, he realised she was naked apart from her skirt, and that was torn from waist to hem. He, too, was in disarray, but felt no shame. Lazily, almost insolently, he ran his gaze over her.

"How do you feel, Pierre? Sleepy?"

"Hungry—very hungry."

She took up a silk dressing-gown, evidently laid in readiness, and wrapped it about her.

She was back within minutes carrying plates and sandwiches.

"*Jambon* there." She pointed. "*Tomates* there."

He pushed a ham roll into his mouth and began to

eat ravenously. Things were beginning to make sense to him.

"Take that thing off!" He indicated the dressing-gown.

Now passionless, she felt some diffidence. She hesitated, then slowly loosened it.

"Right off!"

Reluctantly, she allowed it to drift to the floor.

"Now come here! Don't keep me waiting!"

She obeyed, but slowly.

He seized her wrist and jerked her on to the divan beside him. Because it pleased him, he was rough, even savage. When he released her, there were bruises on her shoulders where his fingers had gripped her fiercely. Struggling to her feet, she faced him angrily.

"There are some things you don't do, Pierre. Hurting a woman is one of them. I only wanted to make you happy."

"You wanted to make yourself happy. That's why you invited me. What do you think I am—a fool. What's more, I'll come here when I like in future."

"You can't." She was breathing heavily, thoroughly unnerved by him. "If the authorities got to know—"

"What do I care about that. Now, where's my ten francs?"

She hurried to find her purse. "If you promise to say nothing about your visit here, and never to come again, I'll give you fifty francs. Fifty, Pierre!"

"Just give me the fifty. Come on!" He thrust out a demanding hand.

She held back. "If I do, you promise—"

"The money!" He interrupted brutally.

She handed it to him, pale and trembling.

"Now, please, dress and go."

"I'm not ready to go yet. I like it here." He sank back on to the divan.

She went on pleading for some time. At last, as if complying with her request, he rose and moved towards the door. She sighed with relief. Turning suddenly, he caught hold of her, his hands snatching at the ties of the dressing-gown with which she had covered herself once more.

"Pierre, no!"

He tore the silk from her with one powerful wrench. Then he flung her on to the divan. His expression warned her of his intentions.

"No, no! Not. . . ." Her protest ended abruptly. She caught hold of his hair and jerked desperately. The pain made his eyes water. He struck her across the face with such force her head sang. She lay limp, while he worked his will on her. She was cold, physically and emotionally, but he was not aware of it.

When he was ready to leave, he had no mercy in his heart for her—no pity. He went out feeling a sense of power. He understood women now. He knew why they had the power to excite and the means to satisfy. They had compelling longings, too. Longings that a man could exploit for his own ends.

He returned home to find his mother waiting for him. His face had a new expression.

"Your supper's ready. I'll get it from the oven."

"I'm not hungry."

She eyed him searchingly. This was not like Pierre.

"Where've you been?"

"Out."

He went upstairs leaving her in a state of worried speculation. Lying in bed, he gave Annette Brujon but one thought. He wondered how she would treat him the following day.

The only visible evidence of her encounter with Molay was on her cheek—a small bruise. He knew there were other marks hidden by her blouse. The thought gave him a peculiar pleasure. Reluctantly, he found himself admiring her. She showed a quite unexpected composure and assurance, and especially with him.

The following week, he deliberately stayed behind after school to be able to speak to her alone. After the rest had gone home, he rose in a leisurely manner and approached her, hands deep in his trousers pockets.

"I'm coming to see you tonight, Annette. Seven o'clock."

"Don't be presumptuous. No one comes to my home unless I invite them—willingly. So whatever time you come I shall not be there."

Astonished, he could find no words to answer.

"I mean that, Pierre. My house will be locked against you. That is all. You may go."

His face flamed. She was actually dismissing him.

"I'm not ready to go."

"Well, I am." She began to stack her books in a neat pile on the side of the desk.

The temptation to catch hold and detain her by force was so great, he trembled. But he dare not do so. There were still several teachers on the premises.

Eyeing him with amusement, she stepped down from the dais and walked slowly towards the door. In those moments he hated her. She had surrendered to him, and he had forced her to bend to his will, yet here she was showing herself to be in command of a

C

situation he had thought to be his. Reaching it, she turned and bid him a polite 'au revoir' before descending the steps into the street.

For the next fortnight that was how things were between them. And then, when he was beginning to think the affair had been a brief, but significant incident in his life, she surprised him more than ever.

"Pierre, you still do not seem to understand fractions. Kindly remain behind after school."

He hardly knew what to make of this. Could it be that she really was anxious to make him understand the sums? Or was it. . . . The second possibility appeared to be too ridiculous for serious consideration. Nevertheless, when they were alone, she came and stood by him.

"I shall be at home this evening—from half-past seven."

He stared, stupefied.

"I'll look forward to seeing you, Pierre. I'll make a really nice supper. Something warm this time. Chicken, fried potatoes and mushrooms."

He nodded, the blood pounding in his temples. He could see that she felt a great physical warmth for him. There were touches of colour in her cheeks. Even now her breathing was a shade quicker than usual.

On the way home, he thought hard about her invitation. Now that she was no longer near, making him alive to her barely suppressed desire and her inviting figure, there crept into his heart a degree of obstinacy.

His hands clenched. Much as he longed to go, he decided against it. Let her make her meal for nothing. Let her wait in growing impatience and frustration. The thought gave him a sense of satisfaction. It helped him to stiffen his resolution to stay away from her.

The following morning as she entered the class-room, she looked at him, her eyes dark with accusation. His upper lip lifted in a sardonic quirk.

After the rest of the scholars had gone home, he sat on at his desk regarding her in a manner that indi-cated all the advantages were his. He knew it was against her will that she came to him, but she came.

"Why didn't you come?"

"Why?" He flung out a careless hand. "Why should I do what you want me to do? Why should I take orders from you?"

"I didn't give orders. I invited. . . ."

"You wanted me, so you *told* me to come to your house. You think you can turn me on and off like a tap. But you'll never do that with me. If I come again, it will be because *I* want it that way."

She drew a deep breath. "But I thought you enjoyed your first visit."

"Then we are both wrong, aren't we."

"Both?" She did not grasp his meaning.

"Yes. I thought you didn't enjoy yourself."

"Oh, but I did."

The confession confirmed his deepest thoughts about her, and about women in general. They enjoyed being made to submit. In the very moments that they were protesting most vehemently, 'No, no, no!' they were desperately hoping the man would go on saying, 'Yes, yes, yes!'

"Will you come tonight?"

He pretended to consider the invitation, but was careful to show no enthusiasm.

"Oh, all right. If you pay me another fifty francs."

She drew back, hesitating. But he knew she would not refuse.

"Very well. Fifty francs."

"There'll be food and wine, too?"

"Yes."

"Then I'll come." His manner indicated that he was doing her a favour.

He was gloating inwardly. His shoulders went back and his chest swelled. *He* was setting the pace. *He* was giving the orders. That felt good.

For his second visit, which proved to be more enjoyable than the first, he made no special preparations. Annette would be only too pleased to have him as he was, being dependent on him for the fulfilment of a desire that overrode every other consideration.

Arriving half-an-hour late, the first thing he did upon stepping inside was to slap her. It was cold, cruel and deliberate. Delivered with the back of his hand when she was turning away from him. There was something terrible in the way he administered it.

She uttered a cry of pain and surprise. But the look on his face told her why he had struck her. It was a reminder that *he* was the ascendant one in their relationship.

Her desire to please was almost abject. She offered everything, including herself, with a sort of eager humility. He took her wine, her food, even her money, with no show of gratitude. Only a sense of lordliness.

At the door, he said: "I'll come again—when I want."

"Yes, yes, Pierre, whenever you wish."

The outcome of that first association with a woman was to be repeated in various ways with all the women who attracted him.

He had only a few weeks more at school before leaving for good, when Annette Brujon failed to report for duty. It was assumed she was suffering from a mild indisposition, and her absence excited no anxiety.

However, when she failed to appear for almost a week, her colleagues decided to make enquiries. It was then that it was discovered that Annette was not in her cottage. The police were notified. The search for the missing woman became more and more concentrated on the river.

Her body was recovered there at midday the following Friday. All the evidence pointed to suicide and the reason for it.

Only two people had the least idea who might be responsible for her condition. Pierre Molay—and his mother.

CHAPTER IV

PIERRE MOLAY gave little thought to Annette Brujon's suicide. He felt no sense of responsibility for her death. After all, it was she who had invited *him* to her home. It was she who had taken the initiative in the affair. She must have known the risks involved. Besides, he had more important things to think about. He was about to start work.

Few boys have said farewell to school with greater satisfaction than did Pierre. The only sphere in which he had done well was in that of physical education. There his advantages were so great, no one could pretend to compete with him. He could out-distance every boy, and out-stay every master in all the races.

In this kind of superiority he had found no satisfaction. Beating a lot of boys who were so much smaller than himself, and so much weaker, he saw was of no consequence. Nor did showing his superiority to his masters give him any satisfaction. Most of them were middle-aged and past their best, anyway.

He knew what work he was to do. His father, displaying a typical French thrift, had left a sizeable nest-egg. And he had stipulated in his will that part of this be set aside for Pierre, to provide him with a business of his own when the time came.

His mother apprenticed him to Albert Durand, who sold and repaired bicycles. In this, she felt she was being far-seeing. Durand, though cursed with a domineering wife, was not blessed with any children, and he was fast approaching sixty years of age. It seemed likely that Pierre would have mastered the various aspects of the business just in time to take over completely from Durand.

Unfortunately, Madame Molay was unable to see what effect the motor-car was to have on the use of the bicycle. The Durands had lived well out of their business, but only because they had reaped the benefit of the years when cycling was at its peak. Even when Pierre was accepted into the workshops as an apprentice mechanic, it was obvious that the bicycle was to suffer an eclipse.

Pierre did not prove himself an apt pupil. Indeed, it was only the fact that he was indentured to the trade, and that the indenture money would have to be refunded, that prevented Durand from sacking him.

Albert Durand confessed that he had made one grave mistake in his life. He had married Gertrude Montanne. During their courting days he had described her, somewhat extravagantly, as 'The Flower of Avigron'. He had not been married to her long before, if he thought of her as a flower at all, it was as a bitter and very noxious weed.

Durand was stout and podgy. His face was much lined and permanently darkened due, no doubt, to the fact that he lived in the perpetual shadow of his wife's presence. He had small hands and a slightly effeminate manner. His eyes bulged and wore a worried look.

If he had been unkind to himself in marrying his 'Flower of Avigron', fate had been equally ungracious in having him with her day and night. The house in which they lived was united to the shop in which he worked and sold his bicycles. At any moment of the day, Gertrude was likely to pop her head round the door from the living-room.

Whatever he was doing, Albert abandoned it and hurried to do her bidding. For Madame Durand had a high-pitched voice. Raised, it had the disturbing, penetrating note of a siren, and was heard far afield. And *Madame* did not hesitate to lift her voice to its piercing, high soprano were she kept waiting.

Gertrude Durand was small and bustling and—at fifty-six or so—decidedly unprepossessing. Perhaps when her husband, in his innocence, had thought of her as a 'flower', she had some claim to good looks. But now, she was bony and her face had fallen in somewhat, and her chin advanced rather too far. And for those who cared to think about her in such detail, her mouth was mean and shrivelled and her nose was beakily narrow, and her eyes were a dull grey. Her hair, had it not been dyed, would have appeared as heavily streaked with white.

She rarely stopped talking, and was one of those women who seemed to be able to pursue her conversation without the need to pause even to draw breath. And most of her conversation was prompted by an inordinate curiosity, or by an abiding sense of disappointment. As Pierre Molay was quick to discover, when Gertrude Durand wasn't asking pertinent, and often highly impertinent, questions, she was bewailing either her own lot or the sad state of France. *Madame* was only happy when she was airing a grievance or ventilating a trouble.

Pierre, quickly becoming aware of the situation in the Durand establishment, marvelled. He told his mother.

"Durand's stupid. He should have cooled that wife of his long ago with a bucket of water. She's impossible. Yes, and she's bad for the business."

She was indeed. She rarely missed knowing who was in the shop, for she peeped round the inner door to see who had entered every time the bell rang. And if she felt the customer could satisfy her curiosity on any point at all, nothing would prevent her asking her question. It needed a great deal of goodwill for a customer to forgive such an impertinence and visit the shop again.

The business would certainly have collapsed had it not been that Albert was an able and conscientious mechanic. He seemed to find in his work the compensations he needed for the indignities, and quite unnecessary worries heaped on him by his wife.

From the first day in the shop, Durand had tried to impress on Pierre the need for accuracy and thoroughness in his work, by trotting out his favourite maxim, 'Good work means good business. Always do the work as if you did each job for yourself. The customer will recognise you as an artisan, and so will come again. What is more, he will tell his friends.' The good advice fell on deaf ears.

Things came to a head the day Pierre was told to replace a bicycle chain which Durand had repaired. This he fitted with a great indifference. Minutes later Durand came over to test it. He lifted the back wheel off the floor and took hold of a pedal. The moment he tried to turn the crank, the chain fell from the gears. Durand's face darkened, his eyes flashed in anger.

"That's it! That's the end!" He surprised Pierre by shouting. "You're finished! I have been patient with you, God knows I have! I've explained to you the same things over and over again. I've taken down and re-assembled work you have done either badly or carelessly. I've known for a long time you were no good here. But I've tried to persuade myself that you will improve. Now, I know I'm wrong. You'll never make a mechanic—never. You're not interested enough. Shiftless and careless! That's what you are, Molay! I should have sacked you long since! But I thought of your poor widowed mother. For her sake I allowed you to remain. But not any longer. You shall go and—"

Pierre shot out a large hand and seized Durand by the lapels of his jacket. He jerked him right off his feet, and shook him as a terrier shakes a rat.

"You runt! Nobody talks to me like that. Why, I'll break every bone in your miserable body."

Durand's face was green with fear. His upper dentures flew from his mouth. He was quite helpless in Molay's hold, and he saw that there was a murderous light in his eyes.

"Albert!"

What the shrill cry did to Durand it is difficult to say. But it so startled Molay he let him go and he slid to the floor. It was only then that he realised just how bad was Durand's condition. For a few moments, he feared he had shaken the life out of his employer, for the face was ashen and the breathing disturbingly quick.

Madame Durand bent over him. Then she darted away, to return with a glass filled with whisky. She poured a little of the spirit down her husband's throat. He sat up suddenly, coughing and spluttering.

"H'm. So you're all right. What have you been up to, eh? Horse-playing about like this—at your age, too! Come now! Tell me! What's it all about? D'you hear me, Albert? What have you been doing?"

"Him—him!" Durand panted, pointing a shaking finger at Molay. "He—he tried—tried to kill me."

"What for?"

It was Molay who answered. "He's decided to sack me."

"What!" *Madame's* head went back with a snap. Her eyes blazed with indignation. "*You* mean to sack *him? You!* Just like that, eh! Without a word to me. How dare you! How dare you!"

Durand was staring, stricken. It had never occurred to him that she might not approve of his action.

"B-but, Gertrude! He's lazy. He's careless!"

"Phshaw! Nonsense! Now, get up, man! Do you hear me, get up!"

Durand scrambled unsteadily to his feet. He retrieved his dentures and went away to wash them.

Madame turned her attention to Molay.

"Take no notice of him. Sack you, indeed! Not if

I know it! Oh, no! I like you. Yes, I like you a great deal. Leave my husband to me. I'll handle him."

She stalked from the shop, shutting the connecting door behind her with an ominous thud.

After a while, Durand came out to him. The man still looked pale and shaken.

"It's . . . it's all right, Molay. Y-you can stay."

"Oh, can I now. I don't know that I want to, not after the things you said."

Durand blanched. He was seized by something akin to panic.

"But you must, you must! If you go, my wife will never forgive me."

"I can't help that. I can't stay unless I can be sure you won't say things like that again."

"Oh, never, never, never! I promise you faithfully."

Molay stared at Durand for a minute longer, subjecting him to the maximum of uncertainty.

"Very well." He returned his hat and coat to their pegs. "But I warn you. Say them once more—just once, mind you—and I walk out. Understand?"

From that moment onward, Molay was virtually his own master in the workshop. What he learnt he did so accidentally, but he did pick up some knowledge of the simpler repairs.

It was Durand who shouldered the responsibility. It was Durand who did the bulk of the work. It was Durand who suffered because of Molay's laziness and domineering manner.

With the outbreak of war, trade declined. With the occupation, it declined still further. Durand was losing interest. He was more and more retreating from life. A Frenchman with a deep love of his country, the return of the Germans was a psychological blow from which he could not recover. Besides, he was suffering another far more insidious occupation—that of Molay.

He dwindled physically and declined mentally. His wife's rantings no longer disturbed him. The time came when he hardly knew what was happening about him. His end was tragic. Unaware that a new stretch of the river had been put out of bounds to the civilian population, he wandered down there one evening. He was challenged, ordered to halt, but did not realise that the guard was addressing him. He continued on his way. There was a flat little explosion. Durand pitched forward, dying even as he hit the ground.

His wife decided to leave the town and go and live with her sister in Dijon.

By this time, Molay was in his twenty-second year. He offered to buy the business. There was, in truth, little to buy, and Madam Durand was pleased to be rid of it at a very nominal price.

And so, although he understood little about the clerical side of the business, Pierre Molay became the owner of the shop and the house attached. To it, the Germans brought all sorts of small repairs. Local residents also came to him with their bicycles when in need of spares. But he often did work that was far below the standards of Durand. He glossed over the shortcomings by reminding his customers that things were difficult, parts and materials were hard to come by.

The excuse was usually sufficient, for the people were well aware of the necessity to make do, to improvise and adapt, and to put up with a multitude of vexations. Molay, in fact, got away with a great deal.

He saw that he would have to get away with a great deal more when the war was over. He knew he would not make a living out of bicycles. In any case, he had no wish to do so. Besides, it was more than a living he wanted, and which he was determined to have.

It was then that Marcel Cavanne made the suggestion that was to have such a profound effect on Molay's life.

CHAPTER V

MARCEL CAVANNE, like Molay, had served in the Resistance. It was through the Movement that the two had first come together. Being an incurable extrovert, Molay had paid little attention to the man. But there were a number of factors on which his lack of perception could have been excused. In contrast to Molay, there was nothing conspicuous about Cavanne except perhaps his ability to make himself inconspicuous. And at that time, with so much else to occupy the thoughts of the Maquis, it had passed unnoticed.

Of below medium height, inclined to be thin, he was pale-faced with mousy coloured hair and slate-blue eyes. His features were so lacking in character as to be readily forgotten.

He spoke little, and when he did say something, he was as economical with words as most Frenchmen are with francs. He never asserted himself in company, being content to sit and listen, cigarette smoke curling from the corner of his mouth as if finding its own unaided way into the atmosphere.

He missed nothing. Nevertheless, he had no watchful look. The guarded expression of the man who was taking in all that was happening around him while, at the same time, conveying the impression that it had no interest for him. Like a jungle animal, he somehow succeeded in mingling with his background, and there he remained smoking endlessly and apparently immersed in his own thoughts. He might have absorbed secrets from the very air, he knew so much.

Women also failed to notice him—until he paid attention to them. Then their awareness of him grew swiftly. They sensed his curious aura of masculinity. To that, they reacted either with fear, departing in haste, or they were as if hypnotised, staying because they wanted to.

Towards the opposite sex he showed a great courtesy. He loved them with a consummate tenderness, as if they were most precious to him. Yet he valued none of them, or if he did, only very briefly.

One woman appeared to be an exception to this—his wife. The men who saw her described her as *la belle dame*. She was tall, deep-bosomed and long-legged. She had broad, powerful shoulders, and a large, smooth face. She was inches taller than her husband, but there was nothing masculine about her.

There was a gentleness in her expression, her eyes held great depths of affection. Her love for her husband was profound, compulsive, and strongly maternal, she soothed him.

It was that which preserved his attachment to her. With other women he found a brief piercing excitement. With his wife he found peace. And his greatest need was to be relaxed. For, despite his outward calm, he was a neurotic and extremely tense. Only he knew it, but he was like a volcano. He appeared to be dormant—even extinct. Inwardly, however, he seethed, even to the point of eruption.

Whether his wife realised this or not, the initiative was wholly hers. She knew, without his breaking the silence, just what it was that he required. She would draw his head on to her bosom, holding it there with one hand while she crooned over him, uttering whispered meaningless words, with the other hand she surreptitiously loosened all his clothing, and, having lulled him into a state of great tranquillity, would lead him unprotesting to bed. Then she would undress, take her place at his side and caress him until he fell asleep asking nothing for herself.

He had no use for men—at least, not socially. He was monkish in his silences, and he had no time for gossip or idle chatter. He was a man who possessed several desperate secrets. His life, certainly his freedom, depended on discretion.

Cavanne presented himself at Molay's bicycle shop one morning. He walked in, the inevitable cigarette in the corner of his mouth, the smoke curling about his face, eyes taking in every detail.

Molay recognised him immediately, but could recall little about him, except that he had been in the Resistance.

"You want a bicycle, *Monsieur*?"

Cavanne shook his head.

"Some spare parts, then, perhaps?"

Again Cavanne shook his head.

Molay eyed him helplessly.

"Then—?"

"Patience!"

Molay stared. He was puzzled. He was also slightly resentful. He was not used to taking commands, not even oblique ones. Yet this man had the air of one who intended to do business.

Cavanne's gaze came to rest again on Molay.

"Business? It is bad?"

Molay was not one to advertise failure, although he had done nothing to ensure the success of the venture.

"Oh, I wouldn't say that."

"*Monsieur, I* would."

"Now, look here—"

Cavanne raised an admonitory finger. It was obvious that he was not intimidated by Molay's bluster.

"I *am* looking, Monsieur, and I am not impressed by what I see. Your trade—it is defunct. Who rides bicycles today?"

Molay was growing more and more curious. This man was obviously here for a purpose—an unusual purpose.

"If you're trying to sell me—"

"I'm not," Cavanne cut in. "I have no wish to sell you anything."

"Then perhaps you will be good enough to explain why you're here?"

"But certainly—at the right time."

Never a patient man, Molay was beginning to feel angry.

"May I point out, Monsieur, that you are on my premises. You come neither to buy nor to sell. But you refuse to say why you are here. Get out!" He began to advance threateningly. "Do you hear? Get out!"

Cavanne stood his ground showing no sign of apprehension. He spoke quietly, choosing his words with studied deliberation.

"If I go I shall not return, and you are likely to lose by my departure—heavily, very heavily."

He gave the unmistakable impression of being the

kind of man who never acted hastily, but who never wasted time.

Molay paused.

"If you have a business proposition to make you had better put all your cards on the table—quickly. I have several matters to attend to."

Cavanne eyed him levelly.

"I think I wish to do business with you. But I must be sure."

"Sure? In what way?"

"I remember you, Monsieur Molay. In the Resistance. That is why I am here. You have courage. You showed yourself to be fearless." His voice changed ever so slightly. "Perhaps you were patriotic."

"I love France, if that's what you mean?"

"More than money?"

Molay hesitated before replying.

"That depends on how much."

"As I thought, *Monsieur*. Like all sensible men, you have your price."

Molay had the unwelcome feeling that this man was mentally far superior to himself. He sensed, too, that he had the more dominant personality. He strove to recall just what part it was that Cavanne had played in the Resistance. To his annoyance, he could remember hardly anything about him.

Cavanne gestured towards the door leading to the living quarters.

"You have someone in there?"

Molay shook his head.

"Good!" Cavanne ejected the butt of his cigarette, stubbed it with his toe and lit a fresh one. "Then I think we can talk. At least, I can. You, my friend, would be wise to listen and to answer my questions."

D

Molay bristled. He hated to have the initiative taken out of his hands. But with this man it might be worth his while to exercise a little self-control. He would soon know. And if he proved to be what Molay was suspicious he might be—a confidence trickster—then he would be thrown out of the shop—after he had been given the thrashing he deserved. Yes, he would be content to wait—a little while!

"My name is Cavanne—Marcel Cavanne."

Molay remembered, then.

"The Faceless One?"

Cavanne nodded.

"I have been called that."

Molay was glad then that he had been willing to listen. There had been whispered stories about Cavanne, although his name had rarely been used. His mother had been dragged from her bed early one morning by the Gestapo, accused of harbouring an Allied airman. She had been forced downstairs, bundled unceremoniously into a truck with others, and done to death some months later in Dachau concentration camp. This, at a time when Cavanne had begun to realise just how much she meant to him.

As a little boy, he had sat for hours on her lap. Madame Cavanne had believed that a child needed above all else to feel secure. That meant, she claimed, that a child should be fussed over and kissed often. Kindness and care for its creature comforts were not enough. It was actual physical contact that conveyed love to a child.

When the news of his mother's death filtered through to him by way of the Underground, Cavanne had reacted by joining the Resistance.

His one motive had been revenge. He had no love

for his country. But he hated the Germans with a terrifying fanaticism that a doctor would have diagnosed as pathological. It accounted for his tension.

It had been rumoured that he had perpetrated many fearful atrocities upon the jack-booted, goose-stepping invaders. Mere killing had failed to satisfy his urge to compensate for the loss of his mother. He had shot his enemies down when that was necessary, time and opportunity allowing him to do no more. But he had dealt with officers and members of the Gestapo in other and far more bestial ways. Some, it had been said, he had sent back to their barracks dumb and blind. Others would never be able to lay claim to manhood again.

All this explained why Cavanne found his wife so essential. It explained why she could give him such a depth of serenity. She had taken the place of his mother. And it was in her vast maturity that he found the ease for his emotions and his conscience.

Molay was now under no illusions as to the type of man who faced him.

"You and I, comrade, we fought for France, did we not?"

"We did."

"And how have we been rewarded?"

"How, indeed?"

"I will tell you. Like beggars. We risked our lives for what? We risked torture for what?" Cavanne spoke without emotion. "For nothing. We made the sacrifice —others are reaping the reward."

"Ah, true! True!"

"Are you satisfied, *Monsieur*?"

Molay spread his hands expressively.

"You, yourself, *Monsieur*. You said I was not doing well. How could I be satisfied?"

Cavanne nodded. "It is as I thought. Like so many others, you have been ignored. However, some of us have sought—and found—means of compensation. Very rich means of compensation. But—" Cavanne left his sentence unfinished.

"Ah!" Molay was beginning to feel a sense of anticipation. At last, Cavanne was about to reveal the real reason for his visit.

Molay's imagination was already busy with the possibilities. Blackmail. There had been no little opportunity for blackmail since the war. So many men and women had been under suspicion of collaboration. Of course, you needed evidence. Concrete evidence of some secret which the victim was terrified would find its way into the light of day. Then, you could pluck your pigeon for all that he had.

It seemed more than likely, however, that Cavanne had something else in mind. The white slave trade, perhaps. Call girls. . . .

"But what?" prompted Molay in an effort to curtail the unduly long silence. "What is your line of country?"

"You need not know that."

"But—"

"For you own sake, you would be wise not to know."

Molay stared, flushing with resentment.

"But if I'm to come in on anything—"

"You'll come in on my terms or not at all. Is that clear?"

Their eyes clashed. Molay was tempted to order Cavanne from his shop. But it was not Cavanne's gaze that fell.

"Please yourself. But the money must be right."

"It will be more than right."

Molay was convinced. But he was unwilling to yield any further ground without knowing more.

"What do I get out of this?"

"Two thousand francs a month."

"Two thousand francs! That is a fairly large sum. Every month?"

"Every month."

"What am I expected to do for it?"

"Receive certain packages. And dispose of them."

"That is all—for two thousand francs a month?"

"That is all."

"The risk must be very great for such a reward."

"Yes, that is what we are paying you for—the risk. But it is not great. If you follow my instructions exactly, you have nothing to fear." Cavanne broke off to light yet another cigarette, his fifth since entering the shop.

There was something compelling about the man. His apparent calm. His unusual assurance. Yet the observant onlooker would have seen in the incessant smoking a symptom of the neurosis which lay behind the immobile features and almost blank gaze.

Molay, however, saw no significance in the habit. He was engaged with other thoughts—more profitable thoughts.

"Where do the packages have to go?"

"To half-a-dozen places—ultimately. But you are only a link in a chain. A very important link, I might add. In fact, it is because we must be most indirect in our deliveries that we need you. That, and something else."

"What else?"

"I will explain that later. At the moment, you simply need to know that the packages will come to Avigron by barge."

"Do I collect them?"

"Indeed, no. That is most inadvisable. The deliveries will be made irregularly, averaging twelve a year. Even so, the authorities will become suspicious if you visit the river to collect the packages from the barges."

"Then—?"

"Do you know Gavroche—Jean Gavroche?"

"Know him? Everybody knows that gutless, little runt."

"You have influence over him?"

"Influence?" Molay's unsupple mind was slow to receive suggestions.

"Could you *persuade* him to act as a courier for you?"

"Oh!" Understanding caused Molay's eyes to glint. "But certainly."

"Good! He works on the river. His presence there should cause no comment—excite no questions. He could receive the packages."

"And pass them to me?"

"Exactly, *Monsieur*. But discreetly. Not the same night that he receives them. He could come here, casually, as a visitor, at times needing his bicycle repairing."

"But he has no bicycle."

Cavanne eyed him rather impatiently. "Couldn't you provide him with a machine?"

"Yes, of course."

"An old one that must always be breaking down and needing new parts?"

"Yes."

"You will be paid for the cycle."

"Gavroche is no longer young. Why would he need a bicycle?"

"Why? What else but to get to his work and return home on it?"

"Ah, yes." Molay found himself unwillingly admiring Cavanne's intelligence.

"He will also be paid. Only a nominal sum, mind you. After all, the risk he will take will not be by any means as great as yours."

"Gavroche take risks! Why, he's a mouse! A shaking jelly of a man!"

"We know all about Gavroche," Cavanne cut in. "It is good that he should be nervous. He will be all the more eager to keep his mouth shut."

"Leave him to me. I'll see he doesn't dare to even think of telling a soul—not even so much as a word to his wife. But she will need watching. She's nosy."

"We know all about Madame Gavroche, too."

Molay detested Cavanne's assumption of superiority. But he was forced to recognise that it was firmly founded. Cavanne knew. Molay began to wonder just how much Cavanne knew about him. Uneasily, he recalled some of his exploits during the Occupation.

"You'll be pleased to know that your trade is to improve, Molay."

"My bicycle trade?"

"That's right. You will find that several people will be calling here to have their cycles repaired."

"But with two thousand francs a month—"

"You will have to earn at least a little of it, *Monsieur* Molay."

Molay nodded unwillingly. It was obvious that these

people would be the contacts whe were to relieve him of the packages. The bicycles they brought would be to guard against suspicion.

"I understand."

"Splendid! But there are some things you do not understand."

"About the contents of the packages, for instance—"

"About that you must guess. No doubt, you will guess correctly in time."

"They are large?"

"On the contrary, they are small. Which explains why we shall find you so useful."

"Useful?"

"Ah, very useful. Allow me to explain. . . ."

And as Cavanne told just what use was to be made of the shop, Molay's eyes widened in wonder.

CHAPTER VI

THE MEETING WITH Cavanne marked the beginning of a new life for Pierre Molay.

Persuading Jean Gavroche to serve as an accomplice had been simplicity itself. The little man had been easily frightened into doing exactly what Molay told him. For Gavroche there had opened a nerve-racking period, to which he could see no end.

He knew his payment was derisory for the services he rendered and the risks he took. But he was not altogether sorry that the payment was so small. His wife was a ferret of a woman. Had he received appreciable sums of money, he would have been sorely taxed to know how to keep them secret from Marie. And had she known he possessed money over and above his normal income, she would have given him not a moment's rest until she had wormed the truth out of him. And then. . . .

Gavroche shuddered when he thought of it. He shuddered even more when he thought what must happen to him if the police ever discovered that he was taking a part—even a minor part—in the business of smuggling heroin.

If ever a man had reason to be unhappy that man was Jean Gavroche. He was caught as it were between the jaws of gigantic pincers. He dare not openly rebel by refusing to continue to bring the heroin. Pierre merely laughed at his fears, and his laugh was not a pleasant thing.

In his soul, Gavroche knew that Molay was a killer. He was just as sure that the big fellow would destroy him if he decided to do so.

As for Molay, he gave Gavroche but scant thought. His life had assumed a sudden ease and contentment. The days of want were behind him. He had entered into a period of the most satisfying fatness.

He knew, of course, that he was handling heroin. The packages brought to him by Gavroche could, he guessed quite early, contain only one thing. He gave the matter no thought. There was a lucrative market for heroin. He was simply one of the agents in the network supplying it. As far as he was concerned, there was no more to it than that.

He did not even trouble to seek justification in the excuse that if he didn't help to meet the need, then somebody else would. Besides, the money he received allowed him the luxuries of wine—the best wines—

and women. And, as far as he was concerned, the women were the best, too.

There had been Antonina, for instance.

Antonina was dark, unusually dark. Her skin was olive, and her hair was as black and as shiny as freshly-hewn coal. Her eyes, too, were sloe and they were knowing.

Molay came upon her in a café known to be frequented by women who were not averse to making money by doubtful means.

Molay was content, usually, with casual acquaintances—men and women. He was suspicious of lasting liaisons. And his contempt for women made it impossible for him to think of ever taking any one of them for a wife.

He eyed her boldly, as he did every woman who caught his attention. She was unusually boyish in build. She had slender hips, and her breasts were obviously small, though perfectly rounded. Her legs, he guessed, were lean and firm and beautifully tapered.

She showed no resentment at his examination. Instead, she smiled, and it was then that he noticed how deeply her mouth curved. Intrigued, he seated himself at her table.

"Alone, *Mademoiselle*?"

She nodded. Her eyes had an amused look. She was patently pleased that she had gained his interest. His presence had this effect on most women. They were flattered that one with such a powerful physique, and of such tremendous aspect, should be drawn to them.

"If you are buying me a drink, *Monsieur*, make it a cognac."

"Did I say I was buying drinks?" He hated to concede even the smallest trifle to any woman. The initiative had to be altogether his.

She began to rise. "In that case—"

"Sit down! I will see to it."

"*Oui, Monsieur.*" She was smiling slyly, provocatively.

Sullenly, he went to the counter and bought two glasses of brandy. Normally, he would have reached out to a woman who behaved towards him as Antonina had done and smacked her across the face. But this girl intrigued him more than most.

"You have a name, *Mademoiselle*?"

"*Oui, Monsieur.*"

When she did not offer to tell him what it was, he demanded impatiently: "Is it a secret, then?"

"Oh, no. It is Antonina."

"Antonina!" It seemed to have peculiarly erotic overtones. He was becoming rapidly more and more intrigued. This girl, ostensibly one of the most sexless, with her leanness, her pointed cheeks and her remarkable air of independence, was firing his blood as no woman he could remember.

He took a long drink of his cognac. She was sipping hers delicately. Her every movement had a rich, unconscious grace. He found himself thinking of a leopardess. She was as lithe as that. Mentally, he had already undressed her.

"You haven't told me your name," she reminded him.

"It is Henri." He never gave his real name if he could avoid it.

"Just Henri? Surely *Monsieur* has another name."

"It is Basque. Henri Basque."

It galled him to see that Antonina was not as

acquiescent as he thought a woman ought to be. His tone was carefully friendly as he asked:

"What is your other name?"

"Sagin."

"You are free tonight?"

"*Monsieur* would like me to be free?"

"Would I waste my time asking if—"

"Ah! You are too quick of temper. You are the hot one, it seems."

"If it's a snowman you want—"

"Oh, no, no, *Monsieur*. But a little courtesy. That is all Antonina wants."

He was sorely tempted to fling the table over and march into the street. The girl was the most impertinent he had ever known. Had he not wanted her so badly. . . .

"Courtesy?" he repeated sneeringly. "What does a woman want with that? Can she eat it? Wear it? Kiss it?"

"Ah, *Monsieur* is a comedian, too?"

If he was, he was feeling particularly unfunny at that moment. He was torn between a fierce desire to knock the smile off her face and the longing to make love to her. His gaze was held by her neck. It was long, smooth, and a pulse at the base of it beat with automatic regularity.

"Are you free tonight? If not, say so, and I will go."

"You are much too impatient. And impatient lovers are most unpleasing."

"No woman I've been with has complained yet."

"Perhaps they were easily satisfied." She was teasing him. "But I—ah, I need finesse. Love is an art, even when there is a fee."

"*Mon Dieu! Mon Dieu!*" He brought his fist down

on the table with a crash that caused both their glasses to leap for the floor. "Do you wish to teach your grand-mama how to suck eggs?"

"Does *Monsieur* see no difference between making love and sucking eggs?"

It was the last straw. He jerked to his feet, his eyes blazing. She dissolved into laughter laying a detaining hand on his arm.

"You . . . stupid . . . man. Cannot you stand a joke? Or is love so serious with you there must be no jesting?"

He did not answer. Instead, he turned and walked towards the door. He was in the street before she over-took him. She ran ahead of him and stood directly in his path.

"Where do you wish to meet me?"

He controlled his temper sufficiently to say curtly: "The Forêt d'Antoinette."

"It is a large place. Just where, and at what time?"

"By the eastern gate."

He calculated quickly. It would be dark by half-past eight.

"Eight o'clock."

"Yes, yes, I shall look forward to seeing you, Henri."

He went home with a feeling of great satisfaction. She had treated him as if *he* were inferior to her. Nevertheless, she had confessed her dependence, in the end, by running after him.

He was deliberately late in keeping the tryst. He was confident she would be there, and just as confident that she would wait for him.

He recognised her in the dusk while he was yet

some yards away. Behind her spread the forest, a great black shadow in the gathering night.

This, he told himself, was as perfect as anything could be. If the proprietor of the café had noticed anything, it would have been of him leaving Antonina in a state of great dudgeon. There was nothing to connect him with the girl.

"You are late, Henri. We agreed to meet on the hour, remember?"

"What of it? It is not yet half-past eight. I'm here now. But if you intend to spend the evening complaining—"

"No, no!" She sighed. "What a one you are for running away. You are not married?"

"No."

"I am not surprised. No woman has ever been given the chance to catch you."

"Nor ever will—if I can help it."

She had tucked her hand through his arm and he was leading her into the wood. It was very dark beneath the trees, but the pale light of the stars penetrated the leaves and branches, revealing the way ahead.

On the edge of the wood, he knew, were other couples. That was why he went so deep into the forest before he halted. He took off his jacket and laid it on the grass in a small clearing. The night was calm and reasonably warm. Only a slight wind infiltrated to where they were, but it was sufficient to set the leaves and grass soughing softly.

He did not allow her to sit down. Instead, he caught her to him. The muscles of her back were hard yet somehow did not impair her femininity. She gasped as the breath was driven out of her, but he did not slacken his hold. He knew well what he was doing. He was sapping her strength, taking all the fight out of her. He crushed his mouth on hers and she beat feebly at him with her fists.

When he finally eased his hold, she sagged and he had to prevent her from falling.

"You—you—" But she could not speak.

"Save your breath, Antonina. You're going to need it."

He laid her down then. She was powerless to resist him.

"Thought you could torment me, didn't you?" he hissed at her through clenched teeth. "Thought you could have me begging—crawling on hands and knees to you. *Mon Dieu*! No woman has ever had me doing that. Cry out! Utter so much as a sound, and I'll beat the life out of you."

He hoped for a whimper of fear, but was disappointed. No sound came from her, although he was sure she was terrified. That was how he liked his women to be. Frenziedly afraid of him.

He was bruising her. Her suppleness was like a too-powerful intoxicant. He embraced her. Her slenderness, so gently curved, was like nothing he had known before. He wanted to absorb her; to reduce her to her essence. Other women had made him feel like this, but none with such a compulsive intensity.

He felt her kicking at him, as if she was alive to the absolute nature of her danger. A pointed shoe caught him smartly on the shin. He grunted, but not with pain. His exclamation was one of sudden, terrible intention.

Antonina Sagin was seized by the throat. He was treating her as no man before him—like a wild beast gone suddenly berserk.

She was agonizingly aware of him now. She could not have repelled him had she wished, and she knew that any hope she had lay in submission. Opposition only served to inflame him more. She made no effort to hinder him.

In vain. As his body began to convulse, his grip upon her tightened. He was impervious to her suddenly bulging eyes; of the protruding tongue, of the slight convulsive movements of her arms and legs. He suddenly became aware of the sighing of the wind. Leaves and grass stirred. But not Antonina. She lay still. Significantly still.

He stared at her in the faint light. He was somewhat startled by her appearance. But he knew just what had happened. He laid a hand on her chest. He could detect no sign of the heart beat. He sought for the pulse he had noticed in her throat. It, too, was still. Antonina Sagin was dead.

He felt no anxiety; no regrets. It was a pity, of course, that she could not serve his purpose again.

For some minutes, he wondered what to do with her. It seemed a simple matter to leave the body where it was. But he knew nothing about fingerprints. Could his be on the girl's throat?

With her stretched at his side, he continued his thinking. Then he remembered the pool in the heart of the woods. It was not too deep, but it was rarely visited, the water being stagnant and dank.

She might lie there a long time before being discovered. And the water would surely wash away any fingerprints there might be.

His mind made up, he began to collect her clothes. These he thrust beneath his shirt. Lifting the body, he slung it effortlessly over his shoulder and began to inch his way forward.

His animal nature stood him in good stead on such an occasion. He was listening all the time, ready to intercept and interpret any sound that might suggest someone was approaching. But he heard nothing.

Reaching the pool, which was almost surrounded by scrub-like bushes, he went to the edge and lowered Antonina's body cautiously into the water. He pushed it hard towards the centre. It went from his sight slowly, a white, shrinking patch absorbed by the black ripples.

Finding a stone, he wrapped the clothes around it and sent the bundle in a wide arc after the body. There was now nothing whatever to connect him with the girl's death. His only problem was to reach home without being noticed. He need not have worried. It was well after ten o'clock, and the people of Avigron tended to retire early.

By the time he slipped through the door of his workshop, he was satisfied he had made the return journey without being seen.

He was hungry. His episodes with women always left him feeling hungry. He was an indifferent cook, but appetite more than made up for his failures as a chef. He made himself a gargantuan meal of fried chops and potatoes. With it he devoured a loaf of broken up bread. He washed it all down with a couple of litres of Rhenish wine. Then he went over to his bed, slung off his jacket and stretched himself out on it.

Within a minute he was sleeping soundly.

E

CHAPTER VII

THE NEXT DAY, after waking late, Molay remembered the incidents of the night before. The mere memory of them was sufficient to set his huge body trembling, as if echoes of his experiences were passing telegraph wise through his every nerve. It was a delight he knew he must repeat as soon as the opportunity occurred—and as soon as it was safe to do so.

He stretched luxuriously, rose, and began to make coffee. It was then, as he turned his thoughts to the more immediate present, that he realised he knew nothing about Antonina Sagin. Last night he had felt no curiosity about her background. Women scarcely ranked with him as human beings. The details of their lives rarely evoked his interest.

Now he realised that who she was, and what she was, might well determine how soon she would be missed, and how thorough the search would be for her.

The evening paper apprised him of the fact that the police had already been informed that the girl was missing. From the report—a brief one—he learned Antonina Sagin had lived with her widowed mother. No mention of her occupation was made. He was surprised when the girl's disappearance suddenly assumed front-page importance. Apparently it was a Press photograph which had sparked off the unexpected public interest. Her striking beauty drawing attention to the fact that she was missing from home.

Madame Sagin had stated emphatically to the

reporters that Antonina was not the type to take her own life, nor was there any reason for her to run away. She was adamant that something had happened to her daughter.

The local *gendarmerie* began to intensify their investigations, but as Avigron was only a smallish town, the forces of law and order were neither large nor particularly bright.

They had, however, a fairly able man in Inspector Faustine Angriz. He was patient and methodical, but he lacked the one quality so essential in the successful detection of crime—imagination. The ability to see beyond the obvious. Besides, the area was difficult to search. There was the river, wide and deep. There were extensive woods, innumerable stretches of waste land.

The resources that could be allocated to look for the missing girl were comparatively slender. Despite the pathetic protestations of her mother, there was no guarantee that she had not gone of her own volition. Nevertheless, what could be done was done, and it proved to be enough. After seven days, gendarmes searching the Forêt d'Antoinette saw the body floating on the surface of the pool.

Things began to happen then with a commendable speed and thoroughness. The girl's clothes were recovered from the bed of the pond. It was established on the spot that the cause of death was manual strangulation, and a post-mortem examination confirmed it. The police began to look for a murderer.

Aware that a manhunt was in progress, Molay was not disturbed. On the contrary, it flattered his ego to think that *he* had set so many men—experts they called themselves, too—chasing shadows.

He was sure there was nothing to connect him with

the Sagin murder—he was right. Hard as it had seemed to find the whereabouts of the girl—or, failing that—her body, it proved an impossible task to uncover a lead as to the identity of her killer. But Molay was well aware that the law had a long arm, and an even longer memory.

It was more than a year before he took any further chances. During the intervening months he stayed clear of the Café Egalité, not wishing to be recognised by the proprietor, and contented himself with less dangerous pursuits.

The girl was in complete contrast to Antonina. Plump, she seemed to do everything at a leisurely pace. Even her facial expressions did not change quickly.

Molay did not approach her. He barely paid her the compliment of a look. She was far from exotic with her obviously peroxided hair and slouched attitude. Arms resting on the table, a cigarette drooping from thickly carmined lips, she was consuming a glass of wine in the most indolent manner possible.

As always, Molay settled himself at a vacant table, but was not allowed to remain alone for long. The girl, after eyeing him speculatively, picked up her glass and lounged over to the chair facing his own.

Without waiting for an invitation she sank on to it. " 'Lo! "

Molay surveyed her distastefully. "I do not know you." His tone scarcely indicated encouragement to remain.

"That is no crime."

Her pertness, so unexpected, aroused his interest.

Nevertheless, at that time, he had no intention of striking up an association.

"My glass is empty, *Monsieur*."

"Then fill it!"

She laughed, not at all perturbed.

"*Monsieur* will give himself the pleasure of paying?"

"It is a pleasure I will allow you to enjoy."

When she persisted in trying to strike up an acquaintanceship, he swore at her viciously, and went from the café in search of another place to drink.

He was surprised to find that her image remained with him during the next few days. He resented it. Why, there was scarcely a redeeming feature about her.

Suddenly he realised that he had never consorted with a woman who was, to say the least, ample. As a rule he liked them slender, with the fullnesses in the right places. That was the only way in which he could explain her fascination for him.

A week later he visited the café again, with but one object in mind. With a sharp sense of disappointment, he saw she was not there. He approached the counter and ordered wine. Using gestures as much as words, he described the girl to the bartender.

"Ah! That is Victoroire, *Monsieur*. Victoroire le Bonn."

"Does she come here often?"

"*Oui*."

"When will she be here again?"

"Today—tomorrow—the day after. Who knows." The man shrugged. "Any time."

Molay asked no more questions. He was content. He only had to wait and the girl would be there again.

But a couple of days elapsed, and his patience was very frayed before she slouched into the café. He gave no sign that he had noticed her entrance but, as he had anticipated, she came over immediately, having already bought a drink on the way.

"So the big one is here again, and still without a guest."

She put down her glass on the table, pulled forward the chair and sat back in it. From beneath lids heavy with mascara, she eyed him slyly.

"*Monsieur* is no gentleman."

Before he could reply, she added quickly, "But, then, I am no lady."

She was telling him—perhaps as she had told scores of other men before him—just what kind of woman she was.

He felt again the uncontrollable urge which had already made him a killer. The compulsion to have the girl was mounting irresistibly, but he dare not visit the Forêt d'Antoinette again for the same purpose. The *gendarmes* were often to be seen in and around that vicinity. They might still be keeping a careful check on couples going into the woods.

He must meet the girl at a different rendezvous.

She arrived at his home long after darkness had fallen.

"You told no one you were coming here?"

"Of course not, *Monsieur*. My clients naturally wish to keep secret their association with me."

"Did anyone see you arrive?"

"No one. I was most discreet."

An hour later Victoroire le Bonn was dead. She died exactly as Antonina Sagin, only she had ended her life in the doubtful comfort of an unmade bed.

He had already considered how best to dispose of the body. In the light of previous experience, he decided that a preconceived plan of action would save time—valuable time.

There was a little used lane linking the street in which he lived with the river. The only serious hazard was crossing this to the head of the track. But he chose his time well. There was no one abroad, not even a drunk, in the whole of the sleeping town.

The girl, although heavier than expected, had not taxed his strength unduly. Wearing thick woollen stockings over his shoes, he carried her half-a-mile almost with only one short rest.

Upon reaching the bank; he slipped her into the river and then silently, like a shadow, went home.

Having carefully brushed his clothes, and removed all traces of mud from his shoes, he prepared a huge *Au Gratin*. It was, he thought as he waited for it to brown under the grill, a sort of *dinner after death. The opposite in a way of the breakfast of the condemned criminal.*

Having eaten his fill, he slept. It was the deep, untroubled sleep usually associated with childlike innocence, or a stainless conscience.

Perhaps Molay was mad, but if so, he showed no sign of it. He was exactly as he had always been.

CHAPTER VIII

THE MURDER OF Victoroire le Bonn came to light quickly. A barge disturbed the waters sufficiently early next morning to bring the body to the surface.

It was only too obvious that this girl had died exactly as Antonina Sagin. It was evident that the hands which had strangled one had also strangled the other.

Molay followed the developments of the case with the air of one watching a macabre entertainment. It was so exciting, when one was in full possession of the facts, to see how stupid the police could be. They were like men groping about in the dark, not even knowing what they were looking for.

He was all the more surprised, therefore, when Inspector Angriz entered his shop some three days after the body had been recovered. With him was a police sergeant, who remained completely silent throughout the interview.

Angriz was what his appearance indicated. He was a plodder. He was thick-set, with a full face and bushy eyebrows. In uniform he would have looked very much like the popular conception of the village *gendarme*. In plain clothes, he looked like a middle-aged artisan on holiday. But he knew his position, and he had an unmistakable air of authority.

"Pierre Molay, I think?"

"And you?" Molay knew who his visitor was, but he preferred to pretend ignorance.

"Inspector Angriz. We are enquiring into the death of a girl named Victoroire le Bonn."

"Well?"

"You knew her?"

"Why, yes, so I do."

"Intimately?"

"No, Inspector."

"When did you last see her?"

"Now let me see—"

Molay's look of reflection was assumed. He remembered well, and he knew exactly what he meant to say.

"Four days ago at the Café Egalité."

"Where did you leave her?"

"Just there, Inspector."

There were other questions, all of which Molay
answered with ease. Inwardly he was laughing. He
knew perfectly well that his position was impregnable.

"Where were you on the night of the twelfth?"

"The twelfth of what?"

"Of the month."

"Where should I be, but here and in bed."

"All night?"

"That is where I stay all night."

The Inspector was trying not to look annoyed. He
disliked Molay. The man had an unpleasant reputation. He was unsociable, sullen and suspicious. He was
also known to be a bully. But such qualities did not
necessarily mean he was a killer.

"Can you prove you were in bed all night on the
twelfth?"

"Can you prove you were, Inspector?"

Molay detested the Inspector's assumption of
authority.

"Do not be impertinent! You are big, but not too
big for us to deal with you."

"You!" Molay's temper was rising. He resented
being quizzed. But to be threatened in addition. . . .

"We are enquiring into a serious matter of murder,"
the Inspector reminded him. "But if you do not wish
to co-operate here we can take you back to the station,
and keep you there until you change your mind."

"You are quite a cockerel when it comes to crowing," Molay sneered, "but this is not *your* midden. You are on *my* premises. What right—?"

"If you wish me to procure a warrant?"

"I wish you to speak to me with some respect. I am not a child. I have a vote. I pay taxes. As a citizen I have certain—"

"I know, *Monsieur*, I know," Angriz sighed.

He had heard of Molay's over-weening vanity. Looking at the man, indifferently dressed, and at the shop, which had such an ostentatious air of decline, he wondered what the man had to be vain about.

"Do you mind if we look round?"

"What do you hope to find?"

"Nothing."

"You can find that anywhere. Why look here for it?"

"To make sure there is nothing to find."

"*Mon Dieu!*" Molay was enraged. "Policeman or no policeman, I will teach you to keep a civil tongue in your head."

The repartee had gone against him. He hated to be made to feel and look inferior. He advanced on the Inspector, his hands balled, his face contorted.

But he never reached Angriz. The sergeant, who until now had been listening intently, moved. He did so in an apparently leisurely manner. But he did so most effectively. Molay found himself pitching to the floor, neatly tripped. He spat out a string of oaths and scrambled to his feet.

The dapper little man allowed him to regain his full upright position. Within a second Molay found himself hurtling through the air. Yet he had no idea how it had happened. He had flung out his hands to seize the uniformed *gendarme*. The sergeant hardly seemed to move. Nevertheless, Molay, big and heavy as he was, was back on the floor.

The Inspector standing well clear, watched the proceedings, his face expressionless.

"When you have had enough, Molay, we will continue."

Molay was now beside himself. He leapt to his feet and charged like a bull. His opponent's hands never left his sides. The sergeant merely shrugged his shoulders, stepped forward and sideways, and Molay was launched head first at the nearest wall.

He hit the plastered brickwork with a sickening thud. Dazed and panting, he lay where he fell. When, at last, he dragged himself to his feet, he knew he was beaten—at least for the moment.

"Do you mind if we look around now, *Monsieur*?"

Molay did not answer.

Minutes later the Inspector rejoined him.

"I do not think that we need to trouble you further. Thank you for your lack of co-operation. Perhaps next time—*Bonjour, Monsieur*."

Molay could not trust himself to speak. He had never felt so humiliated and frustrated. There was murder in his heart. He was sweating with the intensity of his hatred.

He was, at the same time, aware that he had, perhaps, been unwise. There was nothing in the shop which could have betrayed his interest in the distribution of heroin. But there might have been. And his obduracy might well have aroused suspicion. Even with the stuff on the premises, there was little likelihood of its discovery. Nevertheless, he had been short-sighted.

If Cavanne learned of what had happened, he would

be furious. He had given the most careful instructions. If the police showed up they were to be treated courteously. If they were intent on searching the premises, then Molay was to help them. He was to appear unconcerned. He was to show them everything—everything, of course, but what they were looking for.

Instead of complying with his orders, he had been thoroughly obstructive. As far as he knew, the police had no idea that the cycle shop was being used as a vital link in distributing the drug to various agents throughout the length and breadth of France. But if their suspicions were aroused, then his attitude might well be remembered.

Molay had cause to be worried. Since Cavanne had paid him two thousand francs a month, life had been pleasant. If he lost it, his income would become virtually nil. Life would be hard, if not impossible. He would be driven to adopt much more hazardous and far less profitable ways of making a living. And Cavanne would be ruthless if he felt he had been needlessly let down by him. He might not be content with a mere dismissal. Molay shivered at the thought of the other far more drastic, and quite final, possibility.

He was not, however, one to worry long. There seemed no chance of Cavanne hearing that he had tried to attack a couple of *gendarmes*. In any case, the Inspector and his sergeant had been investigating a murder, not searching for heroin.

Nevertheless, Molay decided he would be less truculent should the police call in future.

However, the police had no intention of visiting Molay's workshop again. Inspector Angriz was baffled by the killing. He was also increasingly worried at his failure to make progress in solving a murder which was so obviously the work of a killer who had already a previous assassination to his credit.

Even that was not the worst. The medical reports on the two dead women were exceedingly disturbing. The wanted man was, as far as it was possible to discover, a pervert—and one of the worst kind. He killed as an essential part of his perversion—in the very moment when he was having communion with his victims.

"God, what a throw-back he is, Dupont! Not an animal, even. But, mentally and emotionally, an insect. A spider."

Sergeant Dupont, who rarely spoke, eyed his superior questioningly.

"Don't spiders do just that? Doesn't one kill the other at the moment of—?"

"But it is the female spider who kills, sir, not the male."

"Ah, yes. So it is. But the position is very worrying. If the killer acts under a compulsion he cannot control, he will kill again."

"Unless we catch him."

"And there is little likelihood of that. We investigated the last months of the life of Antonina Sagin. We found that she had been seen with quite a lot of men. We have done the same with Victoroire le Bonn. Again, the list is a long one. But only two names appear on both lists, and neither man has the strength to kill as this monster does. Besides, both have perfect alibis."

"So, *Patron*."

"I must consult the Sûreté. I have no choice. If there is a third killing, there will be an outcry that will be

heard right across France. I must be able to show that
I did everything I could under the circumstances. Put
a call through to Inspector Lotti and ask him to see
me at his earliest convenience on a matter of the
gravest importance."

That same day, having left Avigron as unobtrusively
as possible, Inspector Angriz, on arrival in Paris, made
his way to *No. 11 Rue Des Saussaies*, the Ministry of
the Interior—also the headquarters of the Sûreté,
where he spent a long time in close conference with
Inspector Lotti. He had the reputation of being the
most thorough and remorseless hunter of men.

To Lotti, a criminal was a criminal. For him it was
as simple as that. To students he would say, "The
children who steal from shops, they break the law.
There are minors who go around in gangs damaging
public and private property. They are still law-
breakers. There are maladjusted men who assault
little girls, and women who live by prostitution. They,
too, are law-breakers. Perhaps some of them are sick.
Perhaps some of them are deserving of mercy. If so,
then let the courts be merciful." It was then that he
came as near to showing emotion as anyone, apart
from his wife, had ever seen him display.

"But you don't need psychologists and psychiatrists
to explain that a criminal is not responsible. If a man
who has committed a crime is insane, then the most
ignorant *gendarme* will see it. Yes, and if he is sane,
then the most ignorant *gendarme* will see that also. Do
you know what, in my opinion, is the best psychologist
when it comes to murder?" His listeners could only
shake their heads. "The guillotine! The gas chamber!
The electric chair! The hangman's rope!"

Then seeing the cold look in his eyes, they would shiver.

"Do not shudder, gentlemen. No State can afford the luxury of a queasy stomach. A man who has suffered Madame Guillotine's cutting caress never commits a murder again."

He would then explain that the purpose of the law was twofold. To apprehend and punish, and to prevent.

For him, that was enough. He left everything else to the subtle minds of lawyers, reformers, and politicians.

He was an impatient listener, especially when he thought his time was being wasted by a needless verbosity. And he was a most searching questioner. Once he felt he was closing the net about a criminal, he would forego everything until his quarry had been caught, if that should prove necessary.

He could exist for days on snatched meals, and three or four nights without sleep. But he was no superman. He drove himself to the limits of endurance, then, with his task completed, he would collapse or, at least, slump. And the Sûreté would not see him again for the greater part of a week.

He listened to Inspector Angriz until he was in possession of the known facts. He remained silent, and apparently withdrawn, throughout the run-down. Even when it was finished, it was some time before he spoke.

"To sum up, *mon ami*, you are lost in a fog of speculation."

"I am afraid so," Angriz admitted.

"Obviously, the two killings are by the same person, but they are widely separated. No doubt, if ever the murderer appears in court, a whole panel of psychologists and psychiatrists will be called to testify that this kind of killer is insane, or, at least, not responsible within the law. They will be quite sure he was mad for a few minutes, but will be unable to explain the fact that the accused was sane for well over a year in between the two murders."

Angriz was not quite sure what he was driving at.

"Psychiatrists look for insanity," Lotti explained, "but not us, Inspector. We search for a sane man. A man of no little cunning, and one possessing unusual strength. So much, at least, we know."

"But that in itself is not very helpful in view of the complexity of the case."

"No, but it narrows the field a little. We seek a man who can carry a woman weighing well over eleven stones at least quite a number of yards. It is a pity we do not know just how far."

"Do you intend to come to Avigron and look into the matter?"

Lotti shook his head.

"Not immediately, no. I am sure you and your assistants have done everything possible in the circumstances. I am just as sure that your murderer is laughing at the law. Of course, if he laughs too loudly we shall hear him. But I think he is too shrewd to make that mistake. I do not think, however, that we have any hope of finding evidence now to convict him."

"But this is terrible—terrible!"

"Most terrible. But we are not quite helpless. There are some things we can do before he strikes again."

Angriz looked rather more hopeful.

"What things?"

"I shall have to consider before deciding just what course we might take."

"And in the meantime, Inspector?"

"In the meantime we have other matters to engage us. At least, you have, Inspector Angriz. In point of fact, the Narcotics Department is preparing a report, a copy of which will be sent to you in due course."

Angriz could not conceal his surprise.

"To me?"

"To you. For a long time they have been trying to discover how heroin is being so widely distributed in France. There is a growing, indeed, a grave concern about the quantity of the drug that is circulating in certain cities, and particularly in provincial towns."

Angriz leaned forward in his chair, his face, for the first time, showing signs of animation.

"Do I understand that Avigron is regarded as an important centre for the distribution of narcotics?"

"That might well be the case. Evidence supporting that view is steadily increasing."

"But how—?"

"We are pretty sure that the stuff is brought to your town by barge."

"But why Avigron?"

Inspector Lotti spread his hands significantly.

"For a very good reason. Who would suspect that Avigron—a small inland town of no special geographical importance—would be used for such a purpose? After all, the great distribution centres are usually the capital of a country, or a major port, but a town like Avigron has other invaluable amenities. It is linked by a waterways to the sea as well as by roads, and it is fairly central to the rest of the country."

F

"That is true," Angriz agreed, "but how do you know all this?"

"The department has an agent—a female agent—working on the case. It seems that she has done some excellent work on a fellow named Cavanne—Marcel Cavanne."

"You have evidence of his guilt?"

"I believe enough is available to put him away for a long time."

"Then why is he allowed to remain free?"

"Because Marcel Cavanne is simply a cog in a large organisation. He is a most important cog, I grant you. But he would be immediately replaced if he were removed, and the flow would then continue without interruption."

"Ah! Now I see. Marcel Cavanne is the one we hope will eventually lead us to all the rest?"

"Precisely."

Lotti was well aware that Angriz was a good *gendarme*. He also knew, that being of peasant stock, he was not gifted with brilliant powers of deduction. But he was painstaking, incorruptible, and, what was more important, he never gave up. Once he had embarked upon a course of action, he followed it through to the end, no matter how exacting it might prove. A man possessing such qualities could readily be forgiven for his slow and, at times, ponderous approach to his problems.

"This female agent you referred to, I take it she—"

"She is easily the most brilliant we have had in Narcotics."

"Splendid!"

Angriz was genuinely glad. When he felt so baffled

himself, it was good to know that someone, some-where, was making progress.

"Although you do not know this, we have been checking on lorries, cars, and other vehicles going out of Avigron. So far, without success."

"Perhaps the river—"

"We have checked on all water craft, too. With the same result.

"Besides, the river is not the complete answer. It can only be used for cities east of Avigron. But the heroin is being delivered in appreciable quantities to cities that lie north, west, south and east, as well as at points in between."

"You have a theory about all this?"

Lotti shook his head.

"That is just the point. We have not."

"Are you sure the stuff comes into Avigron?"

"We are certain."

"What about individuals? Could they not be carrying it out hidden about their person?"

"They could, and it may be that some does get out in that way. But by no means all. We have checked on regular visitors who walk into Avigron and out again. But without anything coming to light."

"So you are convinced that vehicles are used?"

"Yes. But so far all we have searched have slipped through the net. That is why we are so baffled. Too much to be carried out by individuals, but nothing to be found on vehicles. We are sure we have overlooked something, somewhere."

Unfortunately, Angriz could make no suggestion as to what it might be.

"As we seem to be groping in the dark," Lotti con-tinued, "we have decided to put you in the picture,

Inspector. You will find all the details in the report. What you will not find is the answer to the most obstinate problem."

"What is the problem?"

"We know that pounds of the stuff are going out of Avigron monthly. But how? That is the problem. Because it is going out in such quantities, those who are responsible for its movement must be fairly frequent visitors to your town. In fact, the idea of using the town has been a stroke of genius. We are sure the organisers have made hundreds of thousands of francs out of this degraded trade. And they look like making hundreds of thousands more. Unless—"

Angriz was feeling rather inadequate.

"What am I supposed to do?"

"Keep a watch on those who visit the town insofar as your forces allow. Also take note of those who leave from time to time, and, if possible, find out where they go."

Angriz nodded. His face was passive, betraying none of his feelings. He had come to Paris to ask for help with one problem—a most pressing one, at that—and he was being told to give his attention to another. Drug peddling was serious. Of that there could be no doubt, but surely it was not as serious as murder.

"But the killings, Inspector, what about those?"

"Oh, I have not forgotten the murders." Lotti assured him.

"Do you think the two things are connected?"

Lotti was emphatic in his reply.

"No, I do not! Indeed, I am firmly convinced that the two are not related. Unless someone in Avigron is taking heroin and it is turning him into a monster. And that I regard as most unlikely."

"Then. . . ?"

"You have two problems, Inspector. Two very big and, as you have pointed out, very urgent problems."

"And I have not the means to deal with them."

"Just so."

"Then. . . ?"

"Leave that to us. We of the Sûreté are as much involved in both these matters as you are. Daily, the Press make us aware of our obligations. What we must decide is how best to tackle them—without frightening off either of the culprits."

Lotti rose and held out his hand.

"You will be hearing from us very soon. That is a promise. Meanwhile, *mon ami*, the best of luck."

Angriz turned at the door.

"*Merci*. I am certainly going to need it, Inspector." And his manner suggested he had little hope that it would come his way.

CHAPTER IX

RETURNING to Avigron, Inspector Angriz gave instructions that all strangers in the town were to be placed under surveillance and reported on. Any who did not appear to have the usual pursuits to engage them were to be subjected to the strictest scrutiny, and would be interrogated by him in person.

The town, although on the river, and pleasant enough in general appearance, was by no means a resort. Avigron only boasted three very modest hôtels, and it was rumoured that even these found it hard to remain open.

Casuals could be broadly divided into two categories.

They were usually either on business, or were visiting relatives. And the majority had associations with the town that immediately absolved them from suspicion.

As Angriz knew that the heroin was transported by barge, he had the river watched, and particularly the stretch where the watercraft tied up at the small quays to discharge their cargoes.

The reports he received daily were numerous, but far from encouraging. No one seemed to meet the barges when they came in from the coast, except those who had been working them for years. There was Jean Gavroche, for instance, but he was merely pursuing his duties in marshalling the barges, ensuring them an accident-free arrival and departure. And he had been doing that for many, many years.

If anyone did haunt the area for nefarious purposes, they did it so skilfully no one detected their presence.

Some of the men operating the barges lived in Avigron, but a thorough investigation showed that none was in any way implicated in the smuggling of narcotics. As for the others, they rarely so much as set foot ashore. There wasn't time.

Various tentative leads were then pursued, but again, without anything of value coming to light.

Angriz was beginning to despair, when he received a report that a woman was staying at the best of the hôtels—the Majestique. She seemed to be alone, and appeared to have no connections at all in the place.

Angriz was intrigued, and all the more so because the report contained the phrase, "She is strikingly beautiful." She had registered under the name of Lucille Evremont, and her occupation was given as "Representative".

The Inspector decided to go along and have a chat

with her. He was happily married, but the idea of meeting a woman who was outstandingly beautiful was a pleasure he was determined not to miss.

From outside, the hôtel looked rather seedy and neglected, being in urgent need of a coat of paint. The interior was no more impressive, but the charges were modest, and it was said that the cooking was exceptionally good. The beds were clean and comfortable.

The receptionist was a man whose expression indicated that nothing could ever again surprise or disgust him, although he appeared to be only in his early thirties.

"Mademoiselle Evremont?" he repeated in answer to the Inspector's question. He indicated the stairs. "First floor, Room 10."

"She's in?"

"I suppose so. Her key is not on the hook."

With Sergeant Dupont at his heels, Angriz went laboriously up. Room 10 took no finding, and the Inspector knocked on the paint-faded door.

When it was opened to him, he could barely suppress a gasp. The girl holding the handle and eyeing him questioningly, was certainly one of the loveliest he had ever seen. She was a natural blonde, with a wealth of golden hair that was most beautifully coiffured. It gleamed with every movement of her head.

Her face was almost heart-shaped, but not quite, so saving her from the 'chocolate-box' type of prettiness. There was character in the mouth, with its soft curves, and in the eyes, which were large, violet-blue, and set wide apart. There were dimples in her chin and in her cheeks.

Her figure was exquisite. She was tall, and it was obvious that her breasts were high and firm, rising richly. Her waist was small, her hips swelling sweetly, her legs were long and exquisitely shaped.

Angriz was middle-aged, and he gave little thought to women. But this woman compelled attention. A look, her merest smile was evocative.

"Mademoiselle Evremont?"

"*Oui.*"

"May I speak to you?"

She regarded him for a long moment.

"I do not know, *Monsieur.*"

"I am from the *gendarmerie.*" He produced his card and handed it to her.

Her eyes widened with interest.

"Ah, a police inspector!" She returned his authority. "Yes, yes, come in. Both of you."

He had never known a greater vivacity. She was incredibly alive. The room was dowdy and dismal in all conscience, but she made it seem far worse than it was. Nothing, the inspector found himself thinking, could detract from her. Nothing would adorn her.

"Please!" Smiling, she indicated chairs. "And you *will* have a drink, of course?"

Normally, being on duty, Angriz would have refused, but he could not say 'No' to such a spontaneous and warm invitation.

"Thank you, yes."

Having poured out three glasses of wine, she handed one in turn to the inspector and his sergeant. Then picking up the third from the tray, she came and perched herself on the arm of a chair. The position brought her skirt riding high above her knees. The sight of her legs was such that the inspector found himself experiencing excitements he had felt were relegated to his past.

Lucille Evremont raised her glass.

"Your good health, gentlemen."

From above the rim she surveyed Angriz devastatingly.

"And what crime have I committed that brings. . . ."

"None, none, *Mademoiselle*." Angriz hastened to assure her. The mere idea of such a beautiful and lively creature being guilty of even the most trivial offence seemed to border on blasphemy.

The long sweeping lashes fluttered provocatively.

"I am glad of that reassurance."

Her skirt had somehow worked its way even higher. He could see the swelling whiteness of her thigh.

"It's just that we would like to ask you a few questions." His throat was dry, and he found it difficult to form his words. She was proving more than equal to thirty years of training, experience, and sophistication. His gaze, in spite of his resolution, kept straying to the shadows above the top of her stocking. *Mon Dieu*! he was thinking. *What a woman*!

"I am at your service, *Monsieur*. I'll be glad to help."

"I'm sure, I'm sure." He felt it an impertinence to be curious about her. He had to remind himself sternly that he had a duty to do. "You are a stranger here, Mademoiselle Evremont?"

"*Oui*, Inspector."

"You are a visitor to Avigron?"

"But of course."

She was nonchalantly swinging a leg. Angriz caught a breathtaking glimpse of lace.

"Would you . . . would you be so kind as to tell me why you are here?" He was actually stammering. All his aplomb and stolid calm had gone.

"Why not, Inspector?" She was smiling, and that gave her the innocence of an angel. But there was that skirt and mind-muddling display of leg. They were extremes, and yet they seemed right in her—a completion of her perfect femininity rather than a contradiction. "I am here on business."

"What sort of business?"

"What sort? See!" She crossed to a case lying on the floor and flung back the lid. It was crammed with various beauty preparations. There were powders and lipsticks and face creams.

"I see, *Mademoiselle*. You are a beautician?"

"You have heard of Armand Jacques, Inspector?"

"I'm afraid not."

"No, no, of course." She laughed, and the sound was like that of perfectly toned bells. "*Monsieur* is a man. But had you been a woman, then you would have heard of the Armand Jacques' 'Josephine' skin range. For months, they have been running a promotion campaign in the principal cities. Now, we are introducing them into the provincial towns."

The firm had been most astute in selecting Lucille Evremont to sell their products, Angriz decided. She needed no aids to beauty, but when it came to making prospective clients aware of their lack of it, nothing could be more effective than the sight of this girl.

"Is the Inspector and his assistant satisfied?"

"We are more than satisfied, *Mademoiselle*."

"I'm so glad." She was bending to close the case. The 'V' of her dress was not particularly low, but low enough to show the white promontories of her breasts.

Angriz felt ashamed to look at them, yet he could not help himself. He had heard of women capable of driving men mad. But not until now had he met one.

She straightened, smiling at him. Was there a know-ing look in her eyes? Had she deliberately made him aware of herself? And if so, why? To suspect her seemed treachery. She was altogether too lovely not to be what she seemed. Or. . . ?

"You intend to remain in Avigron a long time?"

"Mmmmmm. A few weeks, maybe. I intend to hold demonstrations, as well as visit shops and salons."

"You mean to be busy."

"Oh, yes. My firm expects me to work very hard. They demand results. Always results."

"Being modern, they will provide every facility, I suppose?"

"Facilities, *Monsieur*?" She raised quizzical eye-brows and her face took on an elfin curiosity that was altogether charming.

"Of course. Assistants? A car?"

"Oh, no. No assistants. No car, either."

"*Mademoiselle* cannot drive?"

"I'm sorry, Inspector, no. I prefer to ride a bicycle."

He stared. Such a mode of conveyance seemed in-congruous for her somehow.

"The exercise—it is so good for my figure." Her expression invited him to look her over.

"So you intend to visit your clients on a bicycle?" He was doing his best to preserve his professional atti-tude. But it was almost impossible with such a figure to divert the mind and tempt the imagination.

"Yes. On a blue bicycle. You or your assistants will probably see me around. I must set the good example. Exercise is a requisite of health. Health is a requisite of beauty. Cosmetics are but an additional aid to beauty."

"I see." He rose to leave. "I wonder, *Mademoiselle,* if you would do something for me?"

"Of course, if I can."

"Would you let me know when you finally decide to leave the town?"

"Indeed, yes, *Monsieur.*"

"Thank you."

Dupont, who, characteristically, had spoken not a word, was already out of the door, when Lucille Evremont said:

"The Inspector—he will visit me again?"

Angriz felt the blood mounting to his face. To be alone with this girl was all any man could wish. But he knew he must refuse. Too many policemen—some of them brilliant—had sacrificed their careers, and their pensions, because they had unwisely mixed business with pleasure.

"I may. With my sergeant, Dupont."

Her smile remained, as sweet and delightful as ever.

"I will look forward to that, Inspector. *Au revoir, Monsieur.*"

"*Au revoir, Mademoiselle.*"

Once more in the car, his sergeant driving, Angriz said:

"Well, what did you think of her?"

"Dangerous, perhaps."

"I thought she was delightful."

"Just so, Inspector. Dangerous! Delightful!"

"I've never seen such a beautiful woman."

"Nor I. But. . . ." Dupont did not complete his remark.

"Well?"

"I don't think she is what she claimed to be."

The inspector was startled. He had been so bemused

by the girl's remarkable loveliness, his professional suspicion had been in a state of almost complete somnolence.

"You think she was deceiving us?"

The sergeant nodded.

"You actually think a girl like her could be mixed up in such a filthy game as the drug traffic? It seems incredible."

"You know my opinion of women, sir." The sergeant, a confirmed misogynist, had nothing good to say about the sex. When someone asked him about Joan of Arc, he had retorted: "She was no woman. She was a man! She fought and killed like a man. But when she was trapped, she expected to be treated like a woman."

One associated all sorts of things with Lucille Evremont. Beauty, kindness, all the joys and delights of love, but not a purveyor of narcotics.

Angriz sighed and slumped again in his seat.

"Naturally, we'll check up on her."

Back at headquarters, he called for the Directory of Businesses. When it was placed on his desk, he drew the huge volume on to his blotter.

"What was the name of that firm Lucille Evremont told us she works for, Dupont?"

"Armand Jacques, sir."

"Ah, yes." Angriz turned the pages swiftly.

A couple of minutes later, he looked up at the sergeant with a pained expression.

"I would never have believed it. Never!"

"Believed what, Inspector?"

"She *did* deceive us." He stabbed a finger at the directory. "There's no such firm as Armand Jacques. No such firm at all!"

CHAPTER X

DURING THE NEXT two weeks, Inspector Angriz was
notified of four or five strangers who were staying in
the town. There was a little man with a puckish air.
He came with a Punch and Judy show. There was a
woman in her middle fifties. There was a youth.

All were cleared on investigation. The man with
the Punch and Judy show was an eccentric, with a
fondness for children, and a desire to entertain. He
was allowed to move on only after *gendarmes* had
taken his puppets apart in a fruitless search for hidden
heroin. The woman, for valid personal reasons, was
keeping her whereabouts secret from her husband.
The youth, who had lost all his near relatives in a
'plane crash, found it impossible to stay long in any
one place.

There was also a second woman who gave her name
as Ophelia Costair. Like Lucille Evremont, she was
staying at the Hôtel Majestique. She came, she said,
from the little seaport of St. Maria. She was big—
unusually big for a woman. Nevertheless, she was well-
proportioned, being rather over six feet in height.
Despite this, she retained a pronounced feminine air.
Her face, although masculine in its bone structure,
revealed an amiability, if not actual tenderness, dis-
counting somewhat the resolution indicated in its
contours. But Angriz gathered a very distinct impression that he would not like to provoke her.

She was most agreeable when he told her who he
was and the purpose of his visit.

"*Monsieur*, it is a pleasure to help you. But, alas, I am an ordinary, simple housewife. How should one like me be able to aid you?"

"It is surprising sometimes, *Madame*, how seemingly innocent information may prove of great value to the police."

"Then ask whatever you wish."

She looked so large, comfortable, and maternal sitting there in her chair. Why, this woman was ideal for soothing and reassuring fretful and frightened children. She was made to take an anxious husband into her embrace and restoring him to his usual calm, confident self.

It was strange that she should evoke in the inspector's mind thoughts like this. Why, he wondered, should she make him feel so sure that she would make such an excellent mother, and such an attentive, understanding wife?

Was it the softness of her voluptuous breasts, the apparent strength of her arms, the capable hands now in repose? Or was it just the gentle expression in the large, pleasant face?

Whatever it was, that was how she impressed him, and he felt he was wasting his time as much as with Lucille Evremont. Only Lucille Evremont had lied to him. It seemed unlikely, but it was just possible that this woman was deceiving him, also.

"Would you give me your home address?"

"Well . . . now, Inspector. . . ."

He was surprised. Instead of giving the instant reply he had expected, she was hesitating.

"It's . . . it's . . . such a delicate matter." She was profusely apologetic. "But I'd rather not. Anything else—gladly, Inspector."

"Of course, you're not compelled to tell me, although the information you give will be treated with the greatest confidence."

She remained silent. He was mystified.

"You're quite sure, *Madame*?"

"Quite sure."

"Very well. Then perhaps you will tell me what you are doing here?"

"Gladly. I was brought up here, *Monsieur*. I was born in the town, and spent my childhood here. Naturally, I have an affection for the place."

"You visit here often?"

"Lord, no! In fact, this is my first sight of the place since I was fifteen."

The Inspector judged Madame Costair to be rather more than forty. Her affection for the town had not been so very strong if she had been able to stay away from it for something like thirty years.

As if divining his thoughts, she said: "Bringing up a family keeps a woman busy. Sentimental journeys have to be postponed, not once but many times, when the children are small, in favour of dreams at the kitchen sink. When they are old enough to fend for themselves it is very different."

"Yes, yes, of course." He was by no means as sure of this woman as he would like to be. Yet he felt annoyed that he could not altogether trust her. Someone as motherly as she was ought to be open and uncomplicated. It was disillusioning to feel that she was capable of duplicity and deceit. "Then you are here merely to look the town over?"

"That's right. It is so nice to see familiar and long remembered places. The house where I was born, for instance. The school I attended."

"Of course. And the friends you once had."

Madame Costair nodded.

"Could you tell me the names of some of them?"

"Alas, Inspector, my friends have moved away or they died during the Occupation."

"Every one of them?"

"As far as I know. I have not been able to trace any. I am extremely disappointed."

After all these years, the Occupation was still being blamed for all sorts of things. It was also still being offered as an excuse for ignorance. The kind of ignorance Madame Costair was professing now. Of course, she might well be telling the truth. The Occupation had brought great changes, and, anyway, thirty years was a long time. Still, to have lived in a place fifteen years—the most impressionable and, in some respects, memorable years—surely there was someone surviving from a period like that.

"I am flattered by your attention. I never thought that I should ever be of interest to the police—and to an inspector, too."

"How long do you intend to stay, *Madame*?"

"I'm not sure. Maybe two or three weeks more."

"Your husband can spare you for so long?"

"He is a very capable man. Ah, he will miss me, if that's what you mean. He will miss me a great deal. But there are daughters who will look after him."

"I see." The inspector moved to the door. "I don't think we need trouble you longer."

"It has been no trouble." She had risen from her seat. Again, as when he first saw her, he was struck by her great physical strength. She had lazy, easy movements that suggested great reserves of power. "Perhaps I can look forward to seeing you again?"

G

"Perhaps, *Madame*. Meanwhile, *au revoir*."

At the reception desk, he said to the clerk: "Your Madame Costair. Has she been here before?"

"I do not think so, Inspector."

"Can't you be sure? Surely you'd remember a woman as impressive as she is?"

"Oh, I'd remember her. But I've only been here three years."

"And she has not been here during that time?"

"Didn't I just say so?"

Angriz strove hard to keep his annoyance in check. This man was always impertinent. Of course, hôtels did not like the police nosing about. They were liable to unearth all sorts of things the management preferred to keep secret. Besides, guests hated to be quizzed, and particularly when they were enjoying their nights together without the blessing of the Church, or the official approval of the State.

"As soon as Madame Costair decides to leave, let me know."

"Is that an order?" The clerk's face was cold with resentment.

"If she leaves and we don't know about it, I'll make things very uncomfortable for you—very uncomfortable indeed." He stabbed a warning finger at the clerk. "Do you understand that? My sergeant certainly does."

The clerk nodded sullenly, but the inspector knew he had made his point. Whenever Madame Costair left town, he would be forewarned. He would then be in a position to intercept and have her searched if she departed under suspicious circumstances.

Driving back to the station, he said to Dupont:

"The Majestique seems to be entertaining some

unusual guests these days. What do you think of Madame Costair?"

"A most pleasant woman."

"That was my impression."

"So was Lucille Evremont, Inspector."

"You think she was deceiving us?"

"I'm sure of it."

"She was certainly keeping what would appear to be quite innocent information. But why?" The Inspector tapped his finger on the dash-board. "Could a woman as maternal as that be mixed up in the drug traffic?"

"Any woman is capable of being mixed up in anything. You, more than most men, ought to know that, Inspector."

"All right, Dupont. We'll assume that Madame Costair is mixed up in the traffic. It doesn't seem she's been helping to get the stuff out of here. As far as we can find out, she's not been in this town since she was fifteen."

"If she *was* here then. I'm sure she was making up much of her story, Inspector."

"Even to that?"

"Why not?"

"Because we can so easily check on her claim. There are school registers still in existence. They must contain the name of Ophelia Costair. There are teachers, too, who will remember her. She must have been a very big girl—far taller than any other in the school. She can hardly have been forgotten."

"Granted. Except that before marriage her name would not be Costair, Inspector."

"Then why should she tell us a pack of lies about which we can readily check?"

"Perhaps because she doesn't care."

The inspector thought about this for some time.

"But that would mean she was innocent," he said at last. "Innocent of any crime, that is. Then why deceive us?"

"Most probably because she's deceiving her husband. Notice how she refused to give you her home address."

"Yes, I think you have a point there. She doesn't want her husband to know she's in Avigron. That can only mean one thing. She's run away from him."

"Or has a lover here?"

The suggestion seemed ridiculous. Madame Costair had not struck the inspector as being a romantic. His impression had been one of a vast motherliness.

"Oh, surely not! After all, it's unthinkable. She's not at all the type."

"No!" Dupont glanced away from the road for a moment to look at the inspector. "Then I will tell you something, sir."

Angriz waited.

"If ever I sought a woman to love me, I'd look for one like Ophelia Costair."

"*Mon Dieu!*" The inspector was incredulous. Nevertheless, he knew that his sergeant was speaking the truth. "In heaven's name, why?"

"I would enjoy the largeness of her embrace. She would enfold me. Shut me in, if you understand what I mean."

The inspector, in his cadet days, had read somewhere about certain men always longing to return to the warmth and security of the mother's womb. Apparently, Sergeant Dupont was one of them. No wonder he showed no interest in women. There could be only one woman for him—his own mother. But he would feel the urge to marry without being able to bring himself to do so. They were a constant source of torment and frustration to him. Creatures he needed, but could not have. It was not surprising he hated them.

"All right. But how can a woman be having an affair in a town she does not know?"

"Her paramour might be joining her soon. He might even belong here. It's an ideal place for illicit love. It attracts so little attention."

The inspector took out a handkerchief and mopped a perspiring brow.

"Except from the undesirable elements for whom it appears to have a considerable attraction. We'll check on her, anyway."

Enquiries were made of the police in St. Maria, and the sergeant was proved to be right. There *was* a Madame Costair, a lobsterman's widow, living in a cottage near the harbour. But she was by no means big. She was barely more than five feet tall.

"You see, Inspector. I told you she was telling us nothing but lies."

"That's the trouble. I don't see. At the moment, as far as this case is concerned, I don't see anything at all."

CHAPTER XI

ON THE MORNING that Lucille Evremont visited Pierre Molay's bicycle shop, he was feeling particularly pleased with himself.

He had every reason for satisfaction. Everything was going perfectly. It was quite obvious that the police had abandoned hope of ever solving the mystery of the murders of Antonina Sagin and Victoroire le Bonn.

The second death had resulted in quite a spate of activity. There had been many comings and goings, with *gendarmes* everywhere. But it had soon died down.

He basked in the satisfying knowledge that he was safe—perfectly safe. Oh, the police might be suspicious. But what did that mean? Nothing! Nothing at all!

He felt, too, that he knew something else. Evidently, fingerprints did not show up on the human body, or else immersion in water washed them away. Had that not been the case, then they would surely have fingerprinted every man in the town. In that way they would have had what amounted to a signature to the murders.

As for anything else, the inspector could only have drawn a blank. There was nothing to connect him with the two dead girls. He realised that he had stumbled by accident on the secret of immunity. His connections with both of them had been so slight as to be no more than casual. The police were no more suspicious of him than of any other man in the town. It was valuable knowledge. For him, it might well be life-saving knowledge. Whenever a woman inspired in him the urge to use her for his more frantic desires, he must act quickly. To have anyone link him with her might well spell disaster.

He was also very happy about the heroin trade. Cavanne had informed him that arrangements were being made to double the amount of the traffic. When that happened, Molay's payment was to be doubled, too. The past lay behind him. The present was safe. The future looked rosy.

If there was a shadow across his path, it was in his failure to find a woman who evoked the delights he had experienced with Antonina Sagin and Victoroire le Bonn. It was true that he was not altogether without a woman. There was Cosette Baptiste. She was proving as pliable in his hands as clay in a potter's. But she was definitely no more than a stand-in. He was making do with her until someone more attractive came along.

That was the state of affairs the morning that Lucille Evremont appeared. He heard the shop door open, and the bell in his living quarters clattered shrilly. He made for his shop.

He halted at the adjoining door, checked by the sight of the girl. He had never seen anyone quite so lovely. And, although her face was astonishing in its beauty, it was her figure that arrested his attention. Mentally, he was already removing the clothes that concealed it. He could visualise the smooth shoulders, the breasts swelling so fully, pendant and yet firm. He could see the flat belly, dimpled and silken, and the shadowy triangle between the hips.

He needed no imagination to picture the thighs, supple and resilient, for the legs visible below her skirt were shapely—perfect.

Her hand rested on a blue bicycle, and the sight of it gave him cause for thought. Was she one of the agents? He would soon know. He advanced towards her.

"*Monsieur* Molay?"

"That's right." She had not yet given the sign. "What can I do for you?"

"It is this tiresome front brake. It will not work."

He was aware that the large, dark eyes were regarding him with interest. His physique was having the same effect on this girl as on all the rest.

"Let me have a look at it, *Mademoiselle*."

She yielded the cycle to him. He examined the brake.

"A couple of new brake blocks will take care of the trouble. These are much worn and do not grip. They could prove dangerous." He was kneeling, and she was standing very close to him. He had a strong desire to pass a hand under her skirt and touch those tantalising legs.

"You can fix them for me?"

"*Oui*. If you wish."

"Now?"

"Within a few minutes."

"Then, if you will allow me, I will wait."

"Please, do so."

He sought out a couple of brake blocks and a screwdriver. Then he set to work. She bent in front of him, as if to get a closer view of the operation. He saw her thighs then—the full, exciting limits of them. He found his hands trembling.

Fixing the blocks took him longer than was necessary. But he was quicker when she rose to her feet and began to look casually about the shop.

He looked up at her. How gracefully she walked, so perfectly balanced, so unconsciously right in her every movement. Without seeming to be aware of the fact, she drew attention to her figure. It was her innocence in this—whether assumed or real—which made her so superbly attractive.

It was hard to tell what kind of a lover she would make. But, with such wide-set eyes, so dark and so deep, with such a richness of bosom and such vitality,

she would be a rare experience. A Cleopatra surely!
Or a Sheba!

Already the determination to possess this girl was
strong within him. There were other women who had
made him feel that he must have them, but few had
inspired in him the fierce longing he was feeling now.
It was in his nerves, and deeper—much deeper. The
need was in his soul.

He could foresee the end of the affair—if it de-
veloped as he intended. It would be unique in its
delight—as unique as it must be fatal for the girl. It
was a pity she could give him his ultimate joy only
once. But that was unavoidable. If he was to know the
incredible delight of fusing life and death—the beginning and the ending—into the one supreme, rapturous
moment of exaltation, and with the loveliest of women,
then this girl must die.

He felt no compunction about it. No regret. She was
to be sacrificed to the unforgettable ecstasy of creation
and destruction at one and the same time. In such
moments he became as the Hindu god, Siva, knowing
the unbelievable, double delight of making and destroying in the same breathless, exultant moment. For
such an experience he would not hesitate to sacrifice
anyone—not even this girl.

"*Mademoiselle* is a stranger to Avigron?"

She had been looking idly at some old cycles. Now
she turned.

"*Oui, Monsieur*. I am here on business." She explained about the beauty preparations and her firm of
Armand Jacques. But he was barely listening. He was
too fascinated by her to pay much attention to anything else. He had mended the defective brake, but

he was pretending to make final adjustments for the sole purpose of keeping the girl with him.

"Your shop, it is quaint."

"*Mademoiselle* thinks so?"

Most people saw it as dusty and dirty, and hardly better than a junk store.

"I do. I have never seen anything quite like it before."

"It is nothing."

"You make a living, selling and mending bicycles?"

"A not very lucrative living."

She was looking intently at some cycle frames hanging on hooks driven into the walls.

"Where are the new cycles?"

He indicated the only new one on the premises.

"Only one?"

"At the moment, yes. It does not pay me to carry a large stock. They soil quickly. You are interested in buying a new machine?"

"My own—" she indicated the blue model he was holding, "it is old. Beginning to cause trouble, you understand."

"Yes, I understand."

He already knew this girl was not part of the narcotics organisation. She had not pushed the left sleeve of her white blouse above the elbow. That meant he could do as he liked about her without incurring Cavanne's displeasure. Cavanne had made it abundantly clear that no one working for him mixed pleasure with business. But the girl would have been an irresistible temptation even if she had been in the pay of Cavanne. No matter what the cost, Molay knew he had to have her.

"I have some recent catalogues. If *Mademoiselle* would like to see them?"

"If I may."

He brought her the catalogues. She laid them on his work bench and bent over, turning the pages and studying the pictures intently. Molay was studying her in even greater detail. Having seen the richly rounded thighs, he was now looking at the pendant globes of her breasts. There was a tingling in his fingers and feet. It was almost unbelievable that a woman as slender as she should have such full, large breasts.

"That one," she said, pointing to an illustration. "That looks a good sturdy model."

"Yes, yes, it is good. Just the thing for rough roads." He hadn't so much as noticed the name of the machine she was indicating. "You would like me to order one for you?"

"Please. In blue."

"Gladly. Delivery will take a few days—say, four!"

"Oh, I can wait."

"Then you'll be here for some time?"

"Oh, yes. In fact, quite a while longer."

He was silently congratulating himself on his immense good fortune. He had no doubt that this girl would react to him as had done so many others before her. He knew he was unwashed and unshaven, and that his trousers were shiny. But his shirt was open to the waist, revealing the deeply muscular chest with its thick mat of curly hair. The muscles of his arms and shoulders bulged through, showing in clear outline against the shirt.

He knew that most women liked their men to be of the earth, earthy. Physique counted for more than polish and cleanliness, and knowing how to love gained far more favours than knowing how to dress. He had seen the men he regarded as dandies. Usually, they had to beg a woman to be kind to them. Whereas he took all they had to give—and more—without troubling to seek their permission. And that had the women crawling to him.

"*Monsieur* would like a deposit on the cycle?"

"No, no. That won't be necessary, *Mademoiselle*."

"And the repair?" She took a purse from her pocket.

"Leave that until you pay for the new bicycle. I will add it to the bill."

"If *Monsieur* wishes."

She was again looking about the shop.

"These frames," she indicated those hanging on the wall, "are they new?"

He nodded absently, too absorbed to care whether or not his answers were accurate. Yet it was obvious that they were not new. Like almost everything else in the shop, the frames had seen some use.

The girl turned her attention to some handlebars.

"Surely these are not new?"

"Oh, no. No!"

"But people buy them?"

"Now and then. Not everyone can afford a new machine."

He realised she was showing quite an interest in his place. Surely not because there was much to hold her attention. Then the truth dawned on his egotistical mind. She was lingering because of himself! That was it. He was confident now that he was to have his moment with her, and he was sure it would be the most ecstatic—the ultimate—moment of his life.

She turned to him, and she was smiling dazzlingly.

"*Monsieur* is busy and would like me to—"

"Oh, no, no!" he hastened to assure her. "My time is my own."

"But perhaps I am offending because I am so curious?"

"*Mon Dieu,* no!"

"The place is charming. Rather dusty perhaps." She spoke apologetically, her eyes slyly inviting. "But so different."

"I'm glad you see it as such."

"*Monsieur* lives here?"

"My name is Pierre. Pierre Molay."

"Yes, I know."

"My friends address me as Pierre. I would like *Mademoiselle* to do the same."

"Why, of course, Pierre. I forget. I am used to the formalities of the big city of Paris. But here everyone is friendly. Is that not so?"

"That is so. No one calls me Monsieur Molay—not unless they mean to pick my pocket."

"And do they do that frequently, Pierre—pick your pocket?"

He laughed. But he had no sense of humour. And he could not remember the last time he had tried to make a joke. That was some measure of how this girl made him feel—light, gay, in the very best of spirits.

"You live here?"

"*Oui.*"

"In the little room there?" She pointed to the door that led to the rear of the shop.

"There, *Mademoiselle.*" A hot thrill of anticipation spilled through him. "If you would like to see. . . ?"

"I'd love to."

He hurried towards the door, but she hung back. He turned and eyed her questioningly.

"If you wish to see—?"

"Oh, but I do! I do! But I fear *Monsieur* must think me—well, impertinent. Asking to see his home like that."

He laughed. It was a sound he made but rarely, and he was almost surprised by it, himself.

"On the contrary, I'm delighted *Mademoiselle* is interested. Not that there is anything to see. I am but a poor man."

"Then I will not intrude."

"It is no intrusion. I insist." He had returned to her and was laying a prompting hand on her arm.

"As *Monsieur* seems so sure." Her dark eyes twinkled her thanks.

He was trembling inwardly. Touching her had been enough to stimulate his nerves to a pitch of delight that made him pant. He was almost frightened of his own reactions.

"I mustn't stay very long. I told the *maître d'hôtel* I would be back to lunch. Usually, I'm not, but as I explained to him, I was only coming here."

"Yes, yes, of course."

He led the way into the room. She looked round at the untidy bed and uncleared table.

"Ah, so *Monsieur* is a bachelor!"

"Yes. *Mademoiselle* thinks that a crime?"

"No, no. But I am surprised. A man like you—so big, so strong—not to be married. Ah, that is a waste, Pierre." She paused, then added impishly: "A very *big* waste."

She quite mesmerised him. She was reacting to him exactly as he had expected. Women were all alike under the skin however beautiful their face and figure.

"You haven't told me your name."

"Lucille. Lucille Evremont."

He placed a tentative arm about her shoulders, ready to withdraw it if she showed the least sign of resentment. But she gave no sign that she noticed it.

"No genuine antiques?"

"I told you. I am a poor man, Lucille."

"Ah, yes. I forgot."

His fingers brushed against the nape of her neck. She looked up at him smiling. His heart expanded. She was not offended. On the contrary, she seemed to be pleased.

"I take it you do a lot of cycling?"

"Oh, yes. A great deal. I use my machine for business and pleasure. The exercise is good."

"For your figure, of course. No doubt, that explains its perfection." He pointedly indicated her bosom.

"Yes, for my figure. And for seeing the sights, too."

"What sights?"

"Places of interest. Ancient and historical buildings. Old churches, castles, cathedrals, shrines, grottoes—things like that."

"There's nothing like that about here."

"So I gather. It is a pity."

He had transferred his arm from her shoulders to her waist. She still did not demur. He allowed his hand to move up slowly. Stealthily, he touched her breast. She might not have noticed.

He was sure now. She was his for the taking.

He turned her to face him. There was in her gaze a smouldering warmth. His arms went about her. He bent and kissed her. Her mouth came to life under his. How easy it all was! And how exciting!

He lifted and carried her across to the easy chair. He sank down into it, the girl on his lap. He kissed her again, this time on the lobes of her ears, on her eyes and cheeks and, then again, on her lips. He felt her shiver.

He, himself, was trembling. His nerves were already in a state of glowing, pulsating anticipation. He tugged the blouse away from its mooring beneath her skirt. He uttered a hoarse little gasp. His over-eager fingers found her breasts.

He bent the girl far back so that his lips might reach her bosom. She uttered a low moan. He sought the fastenings of her skirt. They eluded him. But she made no effort to help him. Neither did she resist him.

The sweat was standing out upon his forehead. His heart was beating mightily and with an unwonted haste. His hand came up under it seeking to explore her thighs. He encountered the hindrance of lace and silk.

At that moment the shop bell set up its insistent ringing. The girl sprang away from him, clutching her blouse about her.

He was shocked by the interruption, which had been so dramatic and unexpected. He was finding it difficult to transfer himself from the frenzied world of his love-making to the prosaic sphere of his shop and business.

It was a translation he made most unwillingly. He was savagely, if silently, cursing the intruder, whoever he, or she, might be.

He held a warning finger to his lips. "Keep quiet," he whispered. "I'll get rid of them quickly."

She nodded.

He strode into the shop in a truculent mood.

His visitor was Cosette.

He had all but forgotten the girl. She was certainly not the type to make a lasting impression on any man,

except possibly one desperate for a woman. Most of
the people who knew her thought of her as *gentille*
which was a polite way of saying she was nondescript.
With Cosette he had spent two or three evenings of
late. They had been pleasant enough, but lacking that
pinnacle of consummation for which he so constantly
craved.

Cosette Baptiste was neatly made, and she had quite
passable features. She was, too, practical and very
domesticated. Anyone wanting a good wife, it was said
in Avigron, might do far worse than marry her. After
all, she was a good cook and a thrifty housekeeper. But
she was hardly more than plain, and she had a rather
self-effacing manner.

Molay knew what kind of lover she made. Had he
given his opinion, he would have said that she made
a very poor substitute for the real thing. She failed
completely to excite his deeper passions and nature. It
was to that fact that she owed her life.

The truth was that he despised her. He despised
most women, but his scorn for Cosette was born of the
fact that she ranked so low in his erotic estimation.
Compared with the woman who waited for him in the
other room, she was of no account.

"Oh!" He made no attempt to disguise his displeasure. "It's you."

She said nothing.

"Well, well! What in the name of Lucifer d'you
want?"

"I—I—I was passing, Pierre. I thought you might
wish to see me."

"Well, I don't wish to see you. I told you I'd let you
know when I wanted you to work for me again."

He was acutely conscious that Lucille Evremont was

H

within earshot. He was murderously angry that Cosette had surprised him at such a moment. She had quite spoilt what was promising to be a most thrilling conquest. Besides, he had given her strict instructions to stay away from his shop until he sent for her. And he loathed women who could not be relied upon to do as they were told.

Although Cosette was no Venus de Milo, she was by no means stupid. She had detected a great deal in Molay's flushed face and aggressive manner. Intuition told her the reason for it. Her eyes filled with tears.

"Pierre, you are not alone, are you?"

"Of course I'm alone."

"Then what is it I hear from your living-room?"

"Nothing! There is nothing to hear. Now, go!"

"Pierre. . . ." Her voice was wheedling.

"Well?" He was all the time shepherding her to the outer door.

"You *will* want me again?"

"Perhaps! Perhaps!"

"Soon?"

"*Mon Dieu!*" Her persistence added fuel to his anger. "Haven't I already said so! Now go! D'you hear? Get out!"

He almost flung her into the street. He slammed the door on her.

He hurried back to the living-room. Before he reached it, Lucille appeared in the doorway. She was fully dressed, ready to leave.

"That stupid woman! Because I give her a little work on occasion, she is always pestering me for more."

"You must find that very annoying. Still, I don't think she'll trouble you again."

She crossed to her cycle, propped against a wall, and took hold of the handlebars.

"You're not angry, are you, Lucille?"

"Angry? Why should I be? The world's full of women who cannot take 'No' for an answer. Come to think of it, it's full of men who are like that, too!"

"Look!" He was desperate to detain her. "You haven't had a glass of wine. You must have one."

"It's too late, now. It's almost lunchtime."

"I shall see you again?" It was a matter of the greatest importance to him.

She pursed her lips.

"You must." He had never before pleaded with a woman for anything. But he was doing so now.

Her face registered indecision.

"I shall be very busy. I have many people to see and—"

"Yes, yes. But you will have *some* free time, surely?"

"A very little. And there is a grotto. It is in the Forêt d'Antoinette. I must see that."

"Why, that's it! I will show you the grotto." He smiled expansively. "You can then see the grotto and me at the same time."

She still hesitated.

"This evening," he urged. "I could meet you by the lane that leads to the grotto."

"Not here, Pierre?"

"I shan't be here. A friend on the other side of town has asked me to deliver him a bicycle."

He was thinking hard. He had taken a big chance in having Victoroire le Bonn at his home. But it would be unwise to have this girl here at night. She had already told the *maître d'hôtel* she was calling at his shop. That provided the connection he was so anxious should not be established. And that was a link which might prove fatal. If she disappeared, the police would centre their enquiries on him. There was, too, the further considerable risk that she might be seen coming to his shop. If she disappeared after that, his position would be dangerous. Her mention of the grotto opened the way for him—if he handled the matter shrewdly.

If he had to take the risk, he would do so. For he had to have this girl, no matter what the cost. But to have the girl, and be safe at the same time, that would be perfect.

"Aren't you busy during the day?"

"Oh, yes. Very busy."

"Then that's the best we can do. I'll meet you by the path that leads to the grotto in the Forêt d'Antoinette."

She said nothing. Apparently she was still debating with herself what to do.

"It is not far. We would soon be there." He could have hated her, in spite of her incredible good looks. To have him almost begging like this! To humiliate him in this way! Other women came running—like Cosette only minutes ago!

"Then we could come back here for supper. Or visit a restaurant. Whichever you prefer."

Her face was beginning to show pleasure at the prospect.

"If we met at eight, it would still be light enough for you to see the grotto. It's really something. Old—really old. And there's an extremely fine statue of the Virgin Mary."

"Very well. Until eight then."

"Good! Good! You'll really enjoy yourself. But I

must first explain just where we are to rendezvous."

He found a map of the town, and after pinpointing the Hôtel Majestique, showed her just where she had to go and the easiest way to get there.

Two minutes later, Lucille mounted her cycle and rode away. He was so intent on her disappearing figure, he failed to see the girl standing on a corner, also watching her departure.

CHAPTER XII

THROUGHOUT THE rest of that day, Molay could barely contain his impatience. He was sure he was to experience a sublimation that would surpass anything he had ever known. It was hard to wait. Particularly when he had little or nothing to do. But he made not the slightest concession to the importance of the occasion, scorning even to change so much as his shirt.

He spent most of the time gloating. He knew exactly what he would do to the girl. He would not take Lucille as most men take a street woman. There would be no undue haste. He would savour everything to the full. He was like a gourmand anticipating a meal of the rarest delicacies. He dwelt on every step in what would be a frenzy of delight. He guessed he would touch the heights of madness.

His nerves had never been more alive. They tingled as he conjured up mental pictures of the girl being sacrificed to his lust. His blood seemed to sing. To have such a beauty helpless in his hands, unaware of the inexorable fate overtaking her, was in, itself, a sort of ecstasy.

All that afternoon, he undressed her repeatedly. He

ate little, as if his whole being feasted on the pictures of a naked Lucille Evremont. He trembled as he felt her quiver in his grasp in her last moments of dread realisation. He felt the moisture dry out of his mouth as he pre-enacted the final scene. He found himself pacing his shop in a fever of impotence. Never before had he been like this.

He knew that this would be by far the longest day of his existence, even though he lived to be a hundred. Nevertheless, he disciplined himself to wait in solitude during those early, long drawn-out, hours of the evening. But it was an anguish to do so.

He was cunning enough to know that he must not be too soon. The girl must be there first. If she was seen waiting, it would not matter. The outer boundary of the Forêt d'Antoinette was frequented regularly, mostly after dark, by lovers or those eager to make love. The lanes skirting it were usually empty. But he realised he must not be seen lingering about the vicinity where he had arranged to meet Lucille Evremont. He was well-known in the town, but even if he were noticed by a stranger, he would not be forgotten. His extraordinary size would have the immediate effect of stamping him indelibly upon the memory. Should that happen, the police would straightway connect him with her, and the consequences might well be serious. Already there was the risk that she might have told someone at the Hôtel Majestique she intended to meet him. That was a chance he had to take. But it meant he must be all the more careful not to have anyone else able to witness against him.

It was after seven forty-five when he allowed himself to leave the shop. He opened the door casually and looked into the street. There was no one.

Within a couple of minutes of locking up, he was in the track that was the sheltered way to the path skirting the Forêt d'Antoinette. He longed to run. Instead, he paused after some moments and looked back. There was still no one in sight.

It would be fully eight o'clock when he reached the rendezvous. His whole being was glowing. Nothing now could deprive him of the supreme joy awaiting him.

He realised now that he had fixed the meeting rather too early. The light was still strong. Then, upon reflection, he saw that such was not the case. He had decided on a time that was just right. Courting couples were unlikely to be near the forest in broad daylight. And he would soon have the girl in the trees where no one could see them, or, if they did, not clearly enough to identify either with certainty.

He was on the edge of the forest now. He looked back from time to time, but there was no one behind him. Nor did anyone pass him coming from the opposite direction. Filled with expectation, he turned the corner that brought him in sight of the point where he had arranged to meet Lucille Evremont.

She was not there.

He had taken her presence so much for granted that he could not believe his eyes. She must be waiting in the shelter of the trees. Molay hurried forward. She was not anywhere to be seen.

Anger and frustration were like a pain within him. This was something he had not so much as imagined could happen. Could it be that she had mistaken the meeting place? Was she in hiding further along the pathway in order to tease him a little?

Convinced that was the reason for Lucille's absence,

he almost ran round the next bend. He could see for a long way ahead, but there was no figure in the distance.

She *had* to be there. Nevertheless, she was not. And it was already well after eight o'clock. Had she been delayed? Yes, yes, that must be the answer. He seized eagerly on the self-deceptive explanation.

He must stay a while longer. It was a dangerous thing to do, but he felt there was no alternative. To gain the enjoyments he had been promising himself since mid-morning he was prepared to take all chances. Indeed, he was willing even to die.

He crouched within the shelter of a clump of bushes, waiting. The minutes went by inexorably, but Lucille Evremont did not appear. Arm-in-arm, an occasional couple came into view and went into the forest.

Molay began to hate the girl. Had he been deceived by her, after all? Was she, at this very moment, sitting in her room at the hôtel sipping wine, amused at the thought of him cooling his heels here? The idea so obsessed him, he could have murdered her just to satisfy his outraged ego.

When darkness began to fall, he knew she was not coming. No one had ever treated him like this before. It was he who had kept women waiting, deliberately tormenting and disappointing them. In the heat of his exasperation, he again pictured himself killing the girl. He had a quite terrible desire to thrash the life out of her.

She had deprived him of what could only have been for him supreme moments. There should have been ecstasy. Instead, there was this blackness. The emptiness. The emptiness of almost unbearable frustration.

If he should ever have the chance to get his hands on her. . . !

Having satisfied himself that there was no one to see him, he left the cover of the forest and began the journey home. Protected by the rapidly deepening darkness, he took little care about being seen. In any case, he was much too angry to worry.

Upon reaching the door of his shop, he turned the key in the lock and went in, kicking it to with a crash behind him.

A girl who had tried to gain admittance just before eight o'clock and found it fastened against her, appeared off a corner facing the premises. Her face was twisted with jealousy. Her hands clenched in her bitterness. She had been betrayed. She knew where Molay had been, and with whom. Woman-like, her greater rage was directed against the girl. She, too, could have killed her in that moment.

For some minutes Cosette kept her gaze fixed on the glass panel that still bore in black lettering the out-of-date inscription: *A. DURAND. Cycle Dealer*, hesitating. It was fear, not jealousy, or anger, that decided her in the end. Unwillingly, her whole being still burning with a nameless anguish, she turned and made for home.

It was midday, on the tenth of May, that Inspector Angriz received a telephone call at his headquarters in the centre of Avigron. It came from the manager of the Hôtel Majestique.

"Inspector, I wish to report a missing person. A woman—a girl really—a Mademoiselle Evremont. The receptionist informs me that she left the hôtel at about seven-fifteen last night. She did not say where she was going, and she hasn't been back to the hôtel since."

Angriz felt a chill pass through him that reached right to his finger-tips.

"I'll be right over."

He put down the receiver and called in his sergeant.

"It's happened again, Dupont."

"Another murder?"

"That remains to be seen. The girl, Lucille Evremont, has been missing for something like seventeen hours. We're going over to the Majestique now!"

"We'd a man, Levante, watching her, hadn't we, Inspector?"

"Yes."

"Has he reported—?"

"No. Get hold of him. Ask him what he knows. I'll go along to the hôtel. Join me there."

The sergeant nodded and went out. Angriz ordered a police car to be made available at once. He was exceedingly worried. It might be that he was being needlessly anxious, but already he had the unwelcome feeling that the girl was dead. The idea appalled him. To kill anyone of such rare loveliness and vivacity seemed somehow more sacrilegious than the usual murder.

A *gendarme* drove him to the hôtel. Angriz hurried inside. The receptionist met him with his usual imperturbable aplomb.

"She left no message," he said in answer to the inspector's first question.

"None at all?"

"I've just said so. If she'd told me where she was going, I'd have asked to go with her. She's the finest bit of—"

"When I require opinions I'll ask for them. What I

need right now is co-operation. Give me the key to her room!"

He passed it over with a languid hand.

"There's one thing I think you ought to know, *Monsieur*."

"Well?"

"If it's of any interest to you, she left the hôtel by the back way."

Angriz, on the point of moving, stopped and stared.

"The back way! Why?"

"She said she was sure there was a man waiting for her at the front."

"A man?"

"Said she was sure he'd been following her all that afternoon."

"So you let her out by the back door?"

The receptionist spread his hands.

"Why not? She was a guest! She's the kind of girl men *do* follow. They pester her to death, I'm sure. I'd do the same myself."

"Yes, of course, given half a chance."

So that was why Levante had made no report. He had not seen her go out, and must have concluded she was still in the hôtel.

Angriz went up the stairs. Searching Lucille Evremont's room did not take long. And it yielded nothing. A look through her cases proved equally unrevealing, beyond the fact that she favoured some very delicate and expensive undies.

Having locked the door, he went down to the reception desk again.

"I'm putting a man on her door."

"On her door!" The receptionist looked a trifle

uneasy. "What do you want to do? Give the hôtel a bad name? The manager won't like that."

"It can't have a very good one as it is."

"But a policeman prowling the corridors—"

"You're afraid it might cramp the style of some of your clientèle?"

"Well, *Monsieur* must know—"

"I'm not interested in what goes on here, except in so far as it might affect Mademoiselle Evremont. I'll tell my man to be discreet."

"The manager—"

"If he proves difficult, I'll show him I can be difficult too. Understand?"

The clerk sighed, his lips pouting resentfully.

"I understand."

"One final point. Did Mademoiselle Evremont leave on her bicycle?"

"No, *Monsieur*."

"I see." He tossed the key to Lucille Evremont's room onto the desk.

"Do not give that to anyone without my instructions."

He passed through the swing doors of the foyer, and stood on the steps. Looking around for his sergeant, he saw the large, imposing figure of Madame Costair. She smiled pleasantly at him on reaching his side.

"Inspector! So you are here again. In your official capacity, I presume?"

"Yes. I'm worried about Mademoiselle Evremont. She has been reported absent from the hôtel."

"Mademoiselle Evremont?" The voice was quietly questioning.

"Don't you know her?"

The woman shook her head.

"She is young and very beautiful."

"Oh!" The large face broke into a smile of recollection. "Yes. I have seen her, two or three times. What a very beautiful girl she is!"

"Have you seen her since yesterday evening at seven o'clock?"

Madame Costair paused to consider.

"No . . . no, I'm afraid not, *Monsieur*. I spent the evening in my room. I had a headache. Nothing much, you understand. But bad enough for me to wish to lie down."

"And you are now yourself again, *Madame*?"

"Quite. Thank you."

He was about to leave, but she laid a detaining hand on his arm.

"You fear for her safety, Inspector?"

"Well. . . ." He hesitated. "Yes, I'm afraid I do."

"Oh!" The motherly face filled with concern. "You fear something has happened to her? Oh, no, no! She is much too lovely for anything to befall her."

"Yes, of course. Excuse me." He had caught sight of Dupont, and already was hurrying to join him.

Before the sergeant could explain, he had cut him short.

"She left the hôtel by the back way. Evidently she thought our man was someone intending to importune her."

"She realised he was keeping an eye on her?"

"So it seems."

"She must be pretty smart, then, Inspector."

Angriz stared at his sergeant for some moments. That was a point he had overlooked. The girl certainly had been quick to realise she was being followed.

"I want every man we can spare out looking for her.

And I want her found—dead or alive. Preferably alive."

"You think that what happened to Antonina Sagin and Victoroire le Bonn has happened to Lucille Evremont?"

"God help me, I do!"

Dupont stared open-mouthed. He had never known Angriz display so much emotion. But, of course, there was so much involved. Not only was the girl missing, but his chief's position, and future, depended on there being no more unsolved murders in the town.

"Perhaps there is a good reason for her absence, Inspector."

"Perhaps! But I'll know no peace until we find her."

And you might know less after we do, the sergeant was thinking, but he said nothing.

Within half-an-hour a score of policemen were making extensive enquiries in and around Avigron.

It was the following night that Gavroche called in at Pierre Molay's bicycle shop. With him he brought some packages. When he came with these packets, he was always in a state of agitation. The mere touch of them unnerved him.

Besides, he was always unwilling to visit Molay. The man was often as not in an evil humour. Even when he was in one of his more agreeable moods, he lost no opportunity to tease Jean Gavroche about his wife. And the heavy sarcasm stung. It was wounding to be the victim of jests and jibes about a wife's coldness, when he so longed to have the sweet contentments she might so easily have provided.

On this occasion, Molay was in the most vicious

mood Gavroche could ever remember. He pushed Gavroche into the back room.

"Come on, Jean! Out with them!"

Gavroche took the packages from the lining of his coat and from inside his trousers. Molay opened a drawer in the ancient sideboard. It was hardly a secret drawer, but it was not evident to the casual eye. It appeared to be part of the solid front, being above the tier of drawers and apparently forming a curved edge to the piece of furniture.

Into this drawer, as far back as possible, Molay put the packages.

"What's the matter with you?" he demanded impatiently.

Gavroche put a shaking hand to his trembling lips.

"I saw her."

"Saw who?"

"The girl." His voice was scarcely above a whisper.

"What girl? For God's sake, man, speak out. That is, if you've anything to say."

"Y-yes, P-Pierre. They took her body from the river. They've been dragging all day."

For some reason he could not explain even to himself, Molay found himself suddenly shocked.

"Who do you mean by *they*? The police? It's they who have been dragging all day?"

"Th-that's w-what I said."

"You didn't! You didn't say who'd been doing the dragging. Get a grip on yourself. Who was the girl?"

"I didn't hear the name quite. It was spoken by the Inspector when they laid the girl's body in the barge. But he didn't say it to me."

Molay seized Gavroche in his large hands and began to shake him.

"What did you hear? What did you hear?"

"Th-the-the first name was Lucille—"

Molay flung him aside. Gavroche, sick from his shaking and very white, staggered against the wall. He leaned against the brickwork weakly, on the verge of fainting.

Molay was staring unbelievingly straight ahead. All day, as on the day before, he had waited, consumed by a dwindling hope and growing impatience. Never before had he waited for a woman. But he had waited for Lucille Evremont, unable to believe that any woman could stay away from him.

Now he knew why she had not arrived. She was dead. An accident, of course. She must have mistaken the way to the rendezvous and, somehow, walked into the river and lost her life. Nevertheless, the explanation did not quite satisfy him. How could she blunder into the river at that hour?

He tried to shrug the death aside. After all, if the girl was dead, that was the end of her. But he had been so fascinated by her, he could not dismiss her as lightly as he had done the memory of Annette Brujon, Antonina Sagin and Victoroire le Bonn. Besides, his expectations regarding her had been unfulfilled. That promise of the greatest of delights had been snatched from him. He became aware of Gavroche, who was still leaning against the wall.

"You're sure the name you heard was Lucille?"

"Oh, yes, yes, I'm sure, Pierre."

"And the second name? Was that Evremont?"

Gavroche's face brightened in recollection.

"Why, yes. That was it."

Molay stared in perplexity. It was strange that an accident—a *fatal* accident—should have happened when it did. When, he wondered, had she wandered into the river? Almost at the time she had arranged to meet him?

Gavroche was watching him nervously. He had never seen Molay look like this. He seemed bewildered somehow. He wanted the few francs Molay gave him for delivering the packets, but there was no move to hand them over. And Gavroche dare not ask for them. In his present mood, Molay might give him another, and a worse, shaking.

Gavroche edged towards the door.

"I'll be going, Pierre."

Molay did not answer. He was puzzled. And for some reason, he was uneasy.

For Inspector Angriz the last forty-eight hours or so had been exceedingly trying. As the hours mounted and no trace of Lucille Evremont was found, he became increasingly convinced that she had suffered the fate of Antonina Sagin and Victoroire le Bonn. That was why on the third day, he had concentrated his search on the river and the depths of the Forêt d' Antoinette.

And the river had yielded the body. Angriz had felt something near to despair on learning of the discovery. He hurried down to the jetty to view the body. There was no doubt about it. The loveliest woman he had ever seen was dead, and it was equally obvious that she had met a violent end. The marks on her throat strongly suggested that she had been strangled.

Angriz, worried and dismayed, raced back to the station. There, he put through an urgent call to Inspector Lotti.

I

"Another murder? Is that what you said? This line is foul."

"Yes! And another woman, Inspector."

"Her name, please?"

"Lucille Evremont."

Angriz was startled by Inspector Lotti's reaction.

"Evremont! Is that what you said?"

"Yes, but—"

"*Mon Dieu! Mon Dieu!* Not her! Not Lucille!"

"You knew her?"

"Knew her? She was acting for us. Narcotics, you know."

The blood ran coldly indeed through the veins of Angriz.

"She—she was attached to the police?"

"She was. A special investigator. In fact, she was one of our smartest agents."

"I take it you'll be coming down to—?"

"As fast as I possibly can. Whoever killed Lucille Evremont must pay. Besides, there's a madman abroad in your town. Anyone who could destroy so beautiful a creature as Lucille Evremont *must* be insane."

"But he is also very cunning, Inspector. Bear in mind this is his third killing. And with the first two at least, he left not so much as the hint of a clue."

"And this time?"

"It's far too early to say. But so far, nothing—nothing at all."

CHAPTER XIII

INSPECTOR LOTTI arrived that same evening, and he was in a grim mood. He sat in Inspector Angriz's office,

his restless fingers drumming incessantly on the edge
of the desk.

"I've not had worse news for a long time, *mon ami*.
I knew Lucille Evremont well. She was not only beautiful, she was highly intelligent, and quite without
fear. What is more, she was dedicated to fighting the
narcotics pedlar. She spared nothing in her determination to bring to justice anyone she could uncover who
was engaged in the traffic."

"It seems she had a reason for taking up Special
Branch work?"

Lotti nodded. "Yes, indeed. You see, she had a
younger sister, Dorette, to whom she was devoted. She
was as lovely as Lucille. Some say she was even lovelier.
A daring, headstrong girl, she was induced to experi-
ment with heroin. She became a confirmed addict. Her
life is in ruins. There is no cure for her. Today she
is in a home shut off from the world."

"And her sister decided to wage war on those who
circulate the stuff? Which explains her presence in
Avigron."

"Yes. She had just completed some excellent work
in the Mediterranean." Lotti ceased drumming. "In
fact she uncovered the traffic in Perpignan so completely, we have been able to trace the course the stuff
takes from the port. It comes to Avigron by barge."

"How did Lucille Evremont manage to discover the
people involved?"

"By employing her charms. Who could resist
them?"

"Ah, who indeed?"

Lotti gestured. "Quite a number of villains have
enjoyed her favours. It is strange to think that one
who was pretending to love was really so filled with

hate. For it was hatred which served as the spur."

"A terrible thing. She was too lovely for that. And now, look what has happened to her. And where do we start to look for her killer?"

Lotti nodded. "Have you no clues at all?"

Angriz shook his head. "It seems she died as the two other girls before her, Antonina Sagin and Victoroire le Bonn."

"You're sure of that?"

"I'm sure all three were strangled, Inspector. It is about the only thing I am sure of."

"H'mmmmm!" Lotti fingered his blue chin thoughtfully. "You have the medical report?"

"Not yet. But I am expecting it at any moment."

Lotti had been eyeing Angriz for several moments. "You're worried, aren't you?"

"Who wouldn't be? I've already two unsolved murders on my hands—brutal and horrible murders. Now, unless I have a lucky break, I might well have a third."

Lotti nodded. Angriz had plenty to worry about. He felt a genuine sympathy for the man. It was rank bad luck for his opposite number in such a provincial area to have a homicidal maniac, and one of exceptional cunning, operating in the district.

In the metropolis, or one of the larger cities, this type of crime was expected and the police well equipped to deal with it. But here, the force lacked the backing of experts. Oh, they could be called in. But that was all too often regarded by the men on the spot as a confession of failure. There could be no doubt that Angriz was in an unenviable position. The local population would soon be demanding his head, unless he could find the killer of the three girls.

A discreet tap on the door preceded the appearance of a civilian clerk. He laid a paper before Angriz.

"Doctor Lescure's report on the Evremont girl, sir. It has only just arrived."

Angriz picked up the sheet of paper as the clerk withdrew.

He nodded as he slowly perused the typewritten page.

"As I thought, Inspector. She was strangled. I saw her soon after they took the body out of—" He stopped speaking abruptly, staring incredulously.

"Something wrong?"

"In a way, yes. I felt so confident— But I must be mistaken."

"If you would be a little more explicit—" prompted Lotti, barely concealing his impatience.

"Lucille Evremont—there was no interference with her."

"Interference?"

Angriz put down the sheet of paper and looked across the desk at Lotti. "Antonina Sagin and Victoire le Bonn were killed, according to all the evidence, while their murderer was in the act of having intercourse with them."

"But Lucille Evremont was not?"

"According to the pathologist, no. Indeed, he asks me to take special note of the fact. See for yourself."

Angriz passed over the paper, and Lotti studied it briefly.

"Which doesn't surprise me half as much as it seems to surprise you."

"But why should it not surprise me?"

"Why? Because I don't believe that the same man killed the three women."

Angriz was staggered. He had been so sure that the three murders were the work of the same person, the possibility Lotti now suggested had never occurred to him.

"The man who killed Antonina Sagin and Victoroire le Bonn was definitely a psychopath. He is quite mad."

"Mad, when he has enough cunning to cover his tracks so perfectly?" Angriz was indignant.

"Acting under a compulsion, but aware that he was breaking the law. Therefore, he took pains to conceal his tracks. But the killing of Lucille Evremont is in quite a different category."

"Oh! And may I ask on what grounds do you make such a firm assertion, Inspector?"

"Certainly! The first two women died to satisfy the lust of a lunatic. But Lucille Evremont was killed because her murderer knew he had to be rid of her."

"Ah, I am beginning to see what you mean. She had found out who it was in this town who was receiving and distributing the heroin. And he killed her to prevent her divulging his secret."

"That is my theory."

Angriz felt no sense of relief. If Lotti's deductions were right, then there was not *one*, but *two* murderers in Avigron. And were two needles easier to find in a haystack instead of only one? He did not think so.

"I don't see how that helps."

"It is not obvious, but it does a great deal." Something very near a smile was curving Lotti's mouth. "You see, we happen to know now how the heroin is being sent out of Avigron."

"And that helps?" Angriz had brought out a packet

of cigarettes. He offered the carton to Lotti. The inspector shook his head.

"More than you appear to realise, *mon ami.*"

"May I learn how?" Angriz lit his cigarette. The weed soothed him even as Lotti's quiet manner served to give him more confidence.

"You must not think that we have been lacking in faith in you. We have not been doing work we might have left safely in your hands. As you know, the narcotics traffic takes in a network that covers many countries. That our enquiries brought us to Avigron is purely accidental. Our agents have been operating in your town for some months. In fact, ever since Lucille Evremont uncovered evidence to prove that the heroin was being brought here by barge."

"You have been trying to find out how it was sent out of the town?"

"We have done more than that. We have discovered the means."

"Then you have done more than we have, I fear. We have searched every kind of vehicle. We have also searched quite a number of individuals—men and women—without success."

"I know. What is more, the Sûreté is aware of how very thorough you have been." Lotti clasped his hands and rested them on the desk. "But there was one kind of vehicle you did not think of searching."

"Oh? And what is that?"

"Bicycles."

"Bicycles?" Angriz stared hard for a long moment.

"You could hardly imagine a more innocent-looking receptacle, could you? After all, it is so open—so naked. But a bicycle can carry a large amount of heroin. A great deal in the frame. More can be hidden in the handlebars."

"But I thought cycles had been searched?"

"Oh, they had. But, you see, the carrying was more cunning than we supposed. We are now convinced that the bulk of the stuff was secreted in the inner tubes, inside the tyres."

"These people are certainly ingenious, Inspector."

"Very ingenious. But we have been working by the method of elimination. This is the modern world—the world of the motor-car, and the speedboat. That is why we concentrated on powered vehicles. When they failed to yield what we sought, and when individuals hiking in the area failed, too, we began to give attention to bicycles."

Angriz smiled ruefully. "Barges and bicycles. Two leisurely means of transport. It's natural to think dope-runners will be in a hurry. You know what I mean—large profits and swift returns. But that apparently was not the aim. Large profits and sure returns—that is the principle on which these people worked. I'm beginning to see now why Lucille Evremont had a bicycle."

"Exactly. It was the means of her contacting anyone who might be interested in the traffic. And her bicycle may well help us to discover the man who killed her."

"Then we're not quite as much in the dark as I feared."

"No, Inspector, we're not." Lotti sank back into his chair, his hands clasped behind his head. "But we're a long way yet from being able to bring in our man. The great work that Lucille Evremont did was to discover that this town was definitely used as the distribution centre. The shrewdness of the kingpin running this traffic is really exceptional, *mon ami*. All that we had to out-match it was the incomparable loveliness and courage of Lucille Evremont. But they were enough. She persuaded one of the operators to divulge to her that the stuff was being shipped to Perpignan. Had she been as virtuous as she was beautiful, I fear she would never have persuaded him to tell her so much. As it was, she spent months working on this man. Not a minute of that time was wasted."

"But if her work was not complete—"

"It was not. But I am determined to complete it for her." Lotti brought a well-kept hand down on to the desk with a sharp thud of avowal. "I owe her that, at least."

"Her cycle. Just what use was she expected to make of it?"

"It was to serve as the disarming means of gaining for her the confidence of people in the town who had any interest in bicycles. But, primarily, she was to use it to make what would appear to be a natural contact with dealers in bicycles. I take it you have such businesses in Avigron?"

"Pierre Molay!"

"Is he the only dealer in town?"

"There is another. A Monsieur Partuit, but he is old. I cannot imagine him being interested in the drug—"

"Nevertheless, he must be investigated. But this Pierre Molay you mentioned. What is he like?"

"He is unpopular. Surly and inclined to keep himself to himself."

"And he makes a living out of dealing in bicycles?"

Angriz flung up his hands. "Oh, no, no! I imagine

he rarely sells a cycle. He repairs them. But his trade must be almost non-existent."

"How does he live?"

"Poorly, too. In a one-roomed dwelling behind his shop."

"I see." Lotti appeared to be disappointed. "He has no expensive vices?"

"He drinks, of course. Heavily sometimes, I think. But he has no other vice—not even that of marriage."

"A quiet person, from all accounts."

Angriz nodded. "I'd say so. Few people bother with him—at least, not socially."

"Nevertheless, he is one of the men Lucille Evremont was bound to be investigating. Dealers first, she was told, and if that fails, then see what you can discover from individuals who own bicycles."

"Is it your belief that it was one of the men she was investigating who killed her?"

"I'm sure of it. I was before I arrived here, but now I'm more convinced of it than ever."

"Why?"

"It seems reasonably certain to me, in view of the doctor's report on Lucille's body. Had she been killed, the victim of the lust of some maniac, then every man in the town would be under suspicion. But the fact that she was simply murdered—the killer making no attempt to interfere with her—that is enough for me. We are not working entirely in the dark or without direction. Because we know Lucille would contact cycle dealers and, if necessary, those owning cycles, we must contact them. It's as simple as that."

Angriz felt a measure of relief. What Lotti said was quite true. But it left the mystery of the two previous murders as far from solution as ever. However, to bring one killer to justice—that, at least, would serve to show that he was as efficient and ardent in his duties as any other police officer in the provinces. It was a pity one man was not responsible for all three. His capture would then put an end to the whole frustrating business.

Lotti pushed back his chair and stood up.

"We will see your Monsieur Partuit first. After all, if we can eliminate him as a possible suspect, then we narrow our field considerably."

"I'm sure Partuit won't be able to help you, Inspector. When do you intend to see him? First thing in the morning?"

"Tonight—now!"

"But it is very late—"

"It is never too late to be working on a crime of this sort. Any man who could kill Lucille Evremont can only be a monster. Besides, I'll know no peace of mind until I've brought him to justice."

"Very well." Angriz picked up the telephone. "Sergeant, have my car sent round immediately."

Two minutes later, the inspectors were speeding through the darkened and almost deserted streets, making for the home of Monsieur Partuit.

CHAPTER XIV

IT WAS AROUND ten the next morning when the two men met again. Inspector Lotti had spent less than twenty minutes with the aged, shrunken, and obviously unenterprising Partuit.

"We'll have a man keep an eye on him. Just to make

absolutely certain. But I don't think he could kill a sparrow. And I'm even more certain that he couldn't carry a woman like Lucille Evremont three feet, much less could he have transported her from the point of the killing to throw her body into the river."

"Unless he had a helper."

"Meaning a wife?"

"She certainly looked a great deal more robust than he."

"Yes. But our information is to the effect that only one man was concerned in the murder. The tracks leave little doubt about that."

"If the ones we examined *were* those of the killer."

"They did lead to the point where the body was taken from the river."

"Yes, that's true. And, of course, I entirely agree with you. But this case has so many unexpected facets. . . ."

"But no impossible features," Lotti interrupted quietly.

"Having all but eliminated Partuit on the grounds of age and physical infirmity, we have reached a unanimous conclusion. A strong man—and *only* a strong man—strangled Lucille Evremont. Judging from your description of him, the second of your suspects seems to be a much more likely prospect."

"Yes, yes. You're right, of course. Do you mean to see Pierre Molay before lunch."

"Yes. The earlier the better, and if he is our man, I'll be fresh to question him. He must be given no chance to get away. I'll call on him myself and take Tulle along. If you are not present he may be less suspicious. Just tell me where he lives."

When Inspector Lotti rejoined Inspector Angriz at

one o'clock, he was looking very thoughtful and more than usually grim.

"You'll be hungry. I'll send out for lunch."

"Make it a big one. I'm hungry all right, although your Monsieur Molay sticks in my gullet."

"Difficult, isn't he?" Angriz spoke over the intercom, giving instructions for a four course lunch to be brought in from a nearby restaurant.

"Difficult! He's unadulterated poison. And what's more, I feel sure he's our man. I've no proof. At least, not yet. But I want his place raiding and taking apart."

"Now?"

"Not just at the moment. Not until I've seen a man called Gavroche."

"Jean Gavroche? You think he's mixed up in the affair?"

"It's possible."

"But he's no better than Partuit. And he's the most henpecked husband in the town."

"I still think he might be a minor cog in the wheel."

"What makes you wish to see him?"

"The simple fact that Molay claims Jean Gavroche spent the evening with him."

"I hardly see how that can help. After all, he's a liar."

"He's a terrible fellow altogether. That's why he'll be so hard to break down."

"If he claimed Gavroche was with him, then he will already have made sure that Gavroche will back up his statement."

"Just so." Lotti's smile was a thin one. "But Gavroche is not Molay."

"I see what you mean. Didn't you get anything out of him at all?"

"Nothing incriminating. But he did say he knew Lucille Evremont."

"He knew her name?"

"He did."

"Which suggests he knew her more than casually."

"Oh, yes. I'm sure of it. Molay's our man."

"I agree with you. But the evidence? What about that?"

"That may provide difficulties, but I'll find what I need if I have to take the town apart brick by brick."

The quiet fierceness of Lotti's manner had Angriz staring. He had been aware of this man's reputation for a long time. Now he understood why he was the most feared investigator in France.

It was said of him: 'He never forgets and he never gives up.'

"Inspector Angriz, I want Gavroche bringing here for questioning."

"You do not mean to visit him in his home?"

"No. Gavroche is the type who will prove less difficult here."

"Of course."

"And we must act fast."

"There is a special need for haste?"

"A very special need. This is not a local matter. Lucille Evremont lost her life because she was threatening one of the largest organisations in Europe. They have already killed three of our investigators."

"Three!"

"Yes. One in Africa. One in Paris. And the irreplaceable Lucille. Word will have gone out that any witnesses there may be are to be intimidated, if not silenced for ever. Every effort will be made to frighten the truth in before we can persuade those who know

t to let it come out. I am already furious with myself.
We might have been satisfied with the facts Lucille
did so much to uncover. With the evidence she provided, we could have pounced. But we decided to
play a waiting game, and bring in every man in the
ring."

"There was nothing wrong with that. After all, a
criminal is a criminal."

"True. But we already knew the identity of the
head of the organisation."

"You have arrested him?"

"By now, I think he will be in custody. Further-
more, I have given instructions that every known member of the ring is to be brought in. I am afraid it will
result in one of the worst scandals France has known
for a long time."

"Why should there be a scandal?"

"Why? Because the head of the organisation is none
other than the Comte D'Anvigon."

"Anvigon! But he has been tipped as a possible
future President."

"Have I not said there will be a terrible scandal?"

Angriz was shocked. His mind boggled at the pros-
pects Lotti's revelation had opened up for him.

"But others will have to deal with that problem,
mon ami. Our concern is to provide unchallengeable
proof of Molay's guilt. And, already, we have talked
too long. You bring Gavroche in. I have business at the
Hôtel Majestique."

"Very good, Inspector."

Barely fifteen minutes later, Inspector Angriz was
at the door of the Gavroches' home. Everything about
was spotless. He could not suppress a slight smile as

he remembered what was said of Madame Gavroche:
'She has two enemies—men and dirt.'

Madame Gavroche herself came to the door. She
drew it back only a few grudging inches. Through the
opening Angriz made out the thin, erect figure, and
the hollow face. The mouth was curved in lines of
permanent disapproval. The eyes were small and suspicious.

She evinced no surprise. Nor did she enquire his
pleasure. She merely waited in hostile silence.

"I am Inspector Angriz."

"The police!" The voice rose thinly. "What do you
want here?"

"I wish to speak to your husband, Jean Gavroche."

"Oh!" The door was opened much wider. "What
do you want with him?"

"Is he here, please?"

"If he has broken the law. . . ?"

"Then the law will punish him." He had heard
stories of how Marie Gavroche treated her husband.

"The law!" Madame Gavroche paused to lend
emphasis to her words. "*I* will punish him. But he
would not dare—"

"*Madame*," Angriz was taking no pains to hide his
impatience. "There is nothing as yet to suggest that
your husband has broken the law. The truth is, if you
will listen to it, that he might well be able to help the
police in a most important matter under investigation."

"*Him!* Help the police!" Madame Gavroche's
laughter was as cold as an east wind on a frozen marsh.
"Why, he couldn't help himself!"

Angriz felt a deepening distaste for the shrew that
confronted him. He knew several wives who were con-

temptuous of their husbands, but none broadcast the fact in this blatant manner. Although he had no personal knowledge of the man, the inspector could not help feeling sorry for Gavroche. Sorry, and rather angry, that he had not resisted his wife's domination.

"Is he here?" he demanded.

"You have not yet told me why you want him."

"*Mon Dieu!*" The usually placid Angriz exploded. "Do you wish me to charge you with obstructing the police?"

Madame Gavroche stared.

"Charge me! Why, you would not—"

"Do not underestimate me. We wish to see your husband on a serious matter. And I have no intention of telling you what it is. But if your husband is here and I go away without him—"

"You mean to arrest him?"

"I mean to take him in for questioning. Now, *is he here?*"

"No." Madame Gavroche made the admission reluctantly. She hated yielding the least advantage to any man. But she knew she would learn from Gavroche all about the matter the moment he came home.

"Then where is he?"

"He is at *le pharmacie*."

"Where?"

"Just round the corner, there."

Angriz turned to move away.

"Inspector!"

He paused, but did not look back at her.

"When will he be home?"

"I do not know. Possibly in twenty years' time. We might put him in prison to give him a little peace."

There was a gasp and the door banged to behind

him. He was really smiling—the first time since learning of the death of Lucille Evremont.

Jean Gavroche was just coming out of the chemist shop as the police car drew up before the door. Angriz eyed him closely. Everything about him betrayed his nervousness and uncertainty.

Of course, there was very little of him. Physically, he must always have been at a disadvantage. But he possessed none of the self-assurance which invariably compensates men of below average height for their lack of inches.

Angriz opened the car door and called to him.

"Monsieur Gavroche?"

Gavroche started. He stepped back, his eyes wary.

"I'm Inspector Angriz!"

Gavroche nodded. He had known the inspector by sight a long time.

"I must ask you to come along with me to the station."

Gavroche's jaw sagged.

"T-t-to the station? But what for? I've done nothing wrong."

"We want to ask you a few questions—that's all."

"Questions? W-what about?"

"Inspector Lotti will tell you that."

The little colour in Gavroche's face vanished. He became waxen white, and he was shaking like an aspen leaf.

Angriz was surprised. No doubt Madame Gavroche had undermined his nervous system, but not to this extent, surely. Did Gavroche know something? Had he broken the law? If so . . . how? *Good God!* The possibility dawned on him like a sudden blaze of light.

Narcotics! Could this little, quivering, terrified creature be a link in the chain?

Angriz remembered the cunning of the organisation in employing innocent means of transport—barges and bicycles. An innocent town—Avigron. And what human being could be more innocent in appearance than Jean Gavroche.

"Get into the car!"

Gavroche hung back.

"Inspector, m-my wife."

"I've already seen her. She knows you're going to the station."

"Oh, no! Oh, no! She'll kill me!"

"At least, not while you're at the station, Gavroche."

Gavroche climbed into the car. Angriz, after seeing his wife, had meant to try and reassure him. Now, he changed his mind.

The ride to the station was a short one. Throughout it Angriz said not a word. Neither did Gavroche. But, from time to time, he whimpered and more than once covered his face with his hands.

On arrival, Angriz shepherded Gavroche to his office. Inspector Lotti was not yet back, but he returned within a few minutes. He seemed satisfied with the results of his visit to the hôtel. But he made no reference to it. Instead, he took his place beside Angriz, facing the wretched Gavroche across the desk.

"I take it you've asked him no questions yet, Inspector?"

Angriz shook his head. Lotti was sizing up the little man, shaking before him and with a hunted—or was it a haunted?—look on his face.

"You know Pierre Molay, Monsieur Gavroche?"

Lotti's voice was quiet, his tone even suggesting patience and kindliness.

"Y-y-yes, *Monsieur*."

"Do you know him well?"

Gavroche nodded.

"For God's sake speak!" Lotti snapped suddenly. "I want answers to my questions. And I want them promptly. Is that clear?"

Gavroche almost fell off his chair.

Angriz, too, was startled by Lotti's unexpected change of manner. But he understood its purpose.

Gavroche licked at dry lips.

"Y-y-yes, sir," he whispered.

"Good!" Lotti clasped his hands and leaned over the desk. "So you know Molay well. What was there between you?"

"W-why, nothing."

"Yet you called on him regularly?"

Angriz stared. He, himself, had no evidence that Gavroche visited Molay. Then he realised. Lotti had no such evidence, either. He was merely bluffing.

"I c-called on him now and then."

"What for?"

"T-to talk, Inspector."

"Oh, no, you didn't! There was another purpose behind your visits, wasn't there?"

Gavroche preserved a terrified silence.

"Wasn't there?" Lotti's fist hit the top of the desk, bringing a cry of alarm from Gavroche.

The little man shook his head.

"You work on the river, don't you?"

"Y-yes, sir."

"You know all the bargemen there?"

"Y-yes."

"One of them handed you parcels or packets from time to time. Don't trouble to deny it. We know you received these parcels."

For several tense moments, Angriz feared that Gavroche was about to faint. There seemed to be something inhuman in bullying such a frightened apology for a man. Nevertheless, the crimes Lotti was investigating were so terrible there could be no compassion for anyone who had a part in them.

"You were handed packets," Lotti repeated.

Still Gavroche said nothing. Obviously, he was more afraid of someone or something than he was of the police.

"Do you know what was in those packets?" Lotti waited, his fingers drumming a hostile tattoo.

Gavroche shook his head.

"So there *were* packets." Lotti's grim expression showed no sign of relaxing. "Oh, we knew there were, Gavroche. And you knew what was in them."

Gavroche's eyes were bulging.

"Heroin!" Lotti almost spat the word at the cringing figure opposite. "Poison! Do you know what happens to a man who falls a victim to heroin? He goes mad unless he dies! Do you realise what you have been doing? You have been making money out of insanity and death!"

"Oh, no! No, no, Inspector!"

"You dare persist in lying to me?" There was suddenly something terrible about Lotti. He had risen to his feet and was leaning over the desk like vengeance itself. Gavroche cowered back, crouching down into his chair, terrified.

"I know you have received these packets," Lotti

stabbed a finger at Gavroche with every word he spoke, "and do you know why I know?"

Gavroche shook a trembling head.

"Martand! Yes, Philippe Martand, himself, told me."

Angriz was surprised. Philippe Martand had been working on the barges ever since he left school.

"You will not see Martand again. He has already been taken into custody. Oh, yes, we have known about him for a long time. So there is no use you keeping silent any longer."

Still Gavroche did not speak.

"How much did you get for delivering those packets?" He spoke more quietly now, realising, perhaps, that he was so terrifying Gavroche he could not speak.

"N-nothing, really, Inspector. It wasn't payment you understand. Sometimes I got nothing at all."

"Nothing at all?"

"Well, a few francs."

"And you got the money from. . . ?"

Again Gavroche took refuge in silence.

"Who from? Pierre Molay?"

Gavroche's tongue darted over dry lips. His voice was a reedy little whisper: "He-he would kill me. . . ."

"Oh, no! Molay will never have a chance to harm you. The law will protect you against him. But you knew what was in those packets."

"No-no. I guessed—that's all."

"You guessed you were passing drugs, but you failed to notify the police? Don't you realise that is a serious offence?"

"But Molay—he threatened to kill me if I so much as breathed a word. Even my wife knew nothing."

Angriz felt a surge of pity for Gavroche. Terrified as he knew he was of his wife, he had been even more afraid of Molay. It was easy to understand why.

"Listen to me, Gavroche," Lotti's eyes were holding the little man's gaze. "You need fear Molay no longer. Whatever harm he has done you in the past, he will never again be in a position to do so. Now, relax. Be easy. All you have to fear is the consequences of not helping the police all you can. Do you understand that?"

Gavroche nodded, but it was obvious that his fear of Molay was not to be dispelled so easily.

Angriz took out a packet of cigarettes. He rolled one across the desk to Gavroche.

"Have a smoke." He spoke gently, reassuringly, as if to a child. "It will help you. Inspector Lotti speaks the truth."

Gavroche transferred the cigarette to his mouth with a hand that was still shaking. When Angriz held a flame to it, he inhaled deeply.

"Now, I want you to think carefully before you answer my next question. It is of the utmost importance that you answer correctly. Your life, and the lives of others, may well depend on it."

Gavroche, who had reduced his cigarette to a soaking, shredding stump waited apprehensively for Lotti to continue.

"You remember the evening of May ninth—last Tuesday evening, don't you?"

Gavroche swallowed hard.

"Where did you spend it?"

"I—I was at home."

"All the evening?"

"Yes, Inspector."

"You never left your house from seven o'clock until ten?"

"I never left the house from seven until eight the next morning."

"Capital! Capital!" Lotti was rubbing his hand under his chin, a sure sign of satisfaction. "You are prepared to sign a statement to that effect?"

"Oh! Must I?"

"Of course."

"But if Molay—"

"Forget Molay from this day forward."

Angriz, anticipating Lotti's needs had already asked over the intercom for a sergeant to bring in a form of declaration, and to bring a clerk with him. Fifteen minutes later, the statement had been typed out. It was read over to him, and he signed several copies.

Lotti turned to Angriz. "You see, *mon ami*, Molay cited Gavroche as his alibi."

"That is so! He made me promise, Inspector, to say I had been with him."

"I realised that. Just as he scared you into handling those packets, so he frightened you into promising you would serve as his alibi for murder."

Gavroche's eyes bulged. "He—he killed Lucille Evremont?"

"He did."

Angriz was surprised by Lotti's boldness in making such a statement. He shared his conviction, but he was not yet sure that all escape routes had been closed against Molay.

"What about Gavroche, Inspector? Do I charge him?"

"Charge him! Book him with being an accessory to the crime of drug carrying."

Angriz hesitated. "There is no question of him being released on a surety?"

"I think not. For his own sake it is better that we keep him in custody."

"You mean to put me in prison!" Gavroche was appalled. "My wife! She—she'll kill me!"

"Oh, no!" Angriz hastened to point out. "You'll be safe from her here. In fact, you'll have some peace, Gavroche. Lots of peace. I'm sure you need it."

"But when I come out—"

"Perhaps Madame Gavroche will have missed you enough to appreciate you more than she seems to do."

"The inspector is right. Look, you can take it easy. And you'll be safe from everybody."

Gavroche's face cleared for the first time since he had been brought into the station.

"Why, yes, I shall be free of her here. It will be a relief. Such a great relief! Not to hear her complaining will be wonderful."

Making the formal charge took only a matter of moments. The inspectors watched him being led quietly away to the cells with amused smiles. They had never seen a man be so glad at being locked up!

"You seem sure of your man," said Angriz as soon as they were alone. "I must admit that I don't feel quite so certain."

"Gavroche's evidence splits Molay wide open."

"If we could rely on Gavroche. But the lawyers won't find it hard to make him contradict himself. Discrediting one as timid as he is will be all too easy."

"No doubt. But you are overlooking other highly important evidence. The drugs. When we take Molay in, we're going to examine every inch of his place, and every minute part of every item in it. I'm sure we shall find some traces of heroin. Certainly enough to prove he was acting as a most important agent in the organisation. That he was an agent we can, of course, already prove.

"Further, Lucille Evremont was in Avigron for the sole purpose of uncovering the traffic here. We know she contacted Molay. It might be that he was warned about her, or it might be that he tumbled to who she was. In any case, he realised she was not what she pretended to be. He arranged to meet her somewhere near the river, strangled her and threw her body into the water. He is obviously strong enough. He had the motive. He had the opportunity. I learnt at the Hôtel Majestique this morning that Lucille mentioned to the receptionist there that she meant to see Molay again. He has put forward an alibi, and already we can destroy it."

The position, as outlined by Lotti, made Molay appear guilty beyond all doubt. Nevertheless, Angriz, always inclined to be pessimistic, was not satisfied.

"When do you intend taking Molay in?"

"This evening. I want a full report on the people we've rounded up so far who've been dealing in narcotics. Then I'm in a position to confront Molay with the full story."

"You don't think Molay will try to run away?"

"We have a couple of men watching him. He wouldn't get far. But I'm sure he won't try. He's far too confident he's covered up his tracks to think he needs to do anything except sit tight."

Angriz nodded worriedly.

"That's why I'm not quite happy about the position. Molay seems so sure of himself."

"That is not his strength, *mon ami*. It's his weakness. He's too confident. Remember, he had the confidence to kill, thinking he could get away with it. And he must have known he was killing a woman attached to the *gendarmerie*. In spite of that, he did not hesitate."

It was a couple of hours later, when they were making ready to arrest Pierre Molay, that they had a visitor. Madame Gavroche. Her arrival was not altogether unexpected. She marched into the station, demanding a word with Inspector Angriz.

Angriz went out to the reception desk to speak to her. Madame was in a flaming temper, and she took no pains to hide it. She was shaking her fist at the inspector as he approached.

"Where is he? What have you done with him?"

"Your husband?"

"Of course! Who else would I be enquiring about. Bring him to me at once!"

"It may be that he does not wish to see you, *Madame*." Angriz' words were quietly uttered, but deliberately barbed.

"Not—not—" She spluttered so much she seemed in danger of choking. "You tell him I'm asking for him. He'll see me!"

"I'll have a word with him." He turned to the man at the desk. "See that Madame Gavroche stays here. And if she tries to make trouble while I am gone, put her out. Forcibly, if need be."

"I will, sir."

He sought out Gavroche in his cell at the rear of

the building. The little man, seemingly quite composed, was stretched out on his bed reading.

"Your wife," began Angriz.

"Here?" Gavroche's composure vanished.

"She wishes to see you. But if you don't wish to see her, you have only to say so."

"I don't wish to see her, but—"

"Then don't."

"When I go home, though."

"That may be months—years! Why worry about that? Besides, do you know what I think?"

"What, Inspector?"

"That she's going to miss you a devil of a lot more than you're going to miss her."

Gavroche stared incredulously. "Her! Miss *me*? Why, she never stops telling me she hates the sight of me."

"She's a woman, Gavroche. A particularly bitchy one. But she'd be lost without you, to whine to."

The possibility caused Gavroche's eyes to widen even more.

"Ask yourself. Who feeds her? Clothes her? Finds shelter for her? Whose money buys her the wine she drinks? The perfumes she uses? Who pays for everything?"

"Why, I do, Inspector."

"And who'll pay for them while you are in prison?"

Gavroche spread his hands, palms upwards. "I do not know."

"Nor does your wife. And what will you miss?"

Gavroche was nodding, and it was plain that he was thinking thoughts he had never dared to entertain before.

"Her whining and complaining. That's what I'll miss."

"And her warmth in bed? Won't you miss that, Gavroche?"

"*Mon Dieu*! Marie! Warm! Not for years has she allowed me to touch her. She's a hard, hard woman, Inspector."

"So you went on your knees. Oh, Gavroche, how foolish of you. You should have swept her into your arms; ignored her protests—made her do your will. Then she would have adored you—worshipped you."

Gavroche was regarding Angriz blankly. "You really mean that?"

"Of course I do. But I have been here too long already. Do you wish to see your wife?"

Gavroche hesitated.

"Come, come! Be a man. Defy her for once."

"Very well." Gavroche's chest swelled a little. "Tell her I do not wish to see her."

"Splendid, Gavroche. It will be a pleasure."

On his way back to Madame Gavroche, the inspector decided to add to the message. It was time *Madame* was taught a sharp lesson.

Her eyes, dark with suspicion, leapt in anger and dismay when she saw that Angriz was alone.

"Your husband sends you a message, *Madame*. He does not wish to see you."

"Take me to him!" She made to get behind the desk. But the *gendarme* was ready for her. He seized and held her.

"That is not all the message. He says he does not wish to see you ever again."

The little eyes popped. The almost lipless mouth gaped. Madame Gavroche strove to speak, but, for the first time since her marriage, words failed her. She squeaked. She gasped. She managed a wild little cry. But not a coherent word did she utter.

"Your husband wants you to know," went on Angriz, enjoying himself immensely, "that he is determined not to come back to you when he leaves prison."

"Does not—" But the only way Madame Gavroche could express herself was in a scream.

It was a tactical blunder. The *gendarme* holding her, shook her fiercely, and the scream ended abruptly. Over the top of her head the two men exchanged glances. Angriz winked.

"Throw her out! And if she ever dares to come here again without being sent for, set the dogs on her."

Madame Gavroche offered no resistance. The inspector was very much amused. There were no dogs —at least, not on the premises. But he was sure Madame Gavroche would not know that. He was equally sure that she would find herself face to face with reality for the first time. Without her husband, she would be helpless. When he came out of prison, she would be glad to have him back—on his terms.

Angriz returned to his office and Inspector Lotti with the satisfying feeling that he had done a fellow man a good turn. And, being French and from peasant stock, he did not overlook the fact that he had done the good without it costing him so much as a centime!

CHAPTER XV

WHEN THEY WENT to collect Pierre Molay they took half-a-dozen *gendarmes* with them. They also took along Sergeant Tulle. The only ones to enter the work-shop, however, were the two inspectors and the ser-geant. The others were posted outside, covering the only exit from the building.

Pierre Molay came out of the living-room. Seeing them, he assumed a disdainful expression, but they were quick to notice that he was uneasy.

He eyed them derisively, waiting for them to speak.

"We've a warrant to search these premises," Inspec-tor Lotti told him.

"What is it you're looking for?"

"I think you already know."

"The ignorant Molay? How should he know any-thing?"

This was one of his many ways of trying to irritate them. At that moment, had they known it, his heart burned with a murderous hate. The last few days had been fiercely frustrating. Nothing had gone right. There had been the disappointing business of Lucille Evremont.

It had been a mysterious business, too. According to the newspapers, the police were convinced that Lucille had been murdered. The papers did not say for what reason. But, although that troubled him, it was the fact that he had so narrowly missed the unspeakable joy of destroying her which rankled with him.

There would have been beatitude in such an experi-ence. Yet he had failed to seize it. Had he told the girl to come to the house, then she must have been his. But *why* had somebody killed her? That was the curious thing. Did the police know? If so, why were they keeping the matter secret?

To his frustration caused by the murder of Lucille Evremont was added the anxiety he was feeling because no one had called to collect the heroin Gavroche had handed over to him. This had never happened before. Always, the day after Gavroche had passed him the packets and he had secreted them in one of the cycles, an agent had called. Molay never knew the man or the woman who came. They gave no name and the same person never came twice.

He had no means of contacting anyone to enquire about the delay. He had never been given Marcel Cavanne's address. Nor had he been told where he might get in touch with any other member of the organisation.

He had stored the packets in the inner tubes of one of the cycles. And the machine was still there, at least a day longer than it should have been. He had stayed awake all night. It was possible that the agent had reason to come under the cover of darkness. But no one had been.

It had occurred to him to destroy the stuff. Surely a change in routine would have been notified to him well in advance. But he felt it would be unwise to act on his own initiative. The stuff was worth a fortune. If he destroyed it, and then an agent came to collect it, he knew he would be made to pay—probably with his life—for robbing the ring of such a large sum of money.

Something, he felt, must have happened. Something untoward and menacing. Had he been sure of this, he would have known what to do. He had decided to wait, at least for a couple more days. And now the *gendarmes* were here with a warrant to search his premises. It was all too obvious that something was very wrong indeed.

"Search away, Inspector," he invited, assuming a

large show of confidence, and motioning towards the living-room door. "Molay does not know what you expect to find, but he hopes you have the good fortune to find it."

"We have no wish to look into your living quarters as yet. May we use your tools, *Monsieur*?"

Molay looked mystified. "Tools? What tools?"

"The tools you use to repair bicycles. We intend to take all your machines to pieces."

Molay's hands clenched. "*Mon Dieu*, no! The bicycles—they are my living."

"Any damage we do will be made good. Now, may we use your tools? If you refuse, we shall use the ones we have brought in the cars."

Molay knew he could not refuse. "Go ahead, go ahead! Waste your time! Ruin me!"

He crossed in a casual manner to the cycle in which he had hidden the incriminating packets. Lotti and Angriz did not appear to be paying him any attention. He bent, picked up a spanner, and began to unscrew the nuts holding the back wheel.

A shadow fell across him. He looked up, to see Lotti standing over him.

"We'll do that, Molay."

Molay was very still for a long second. Then he stood up. He said nothing, but moved away.

Inspector Lotti went to work on the cycle, showing an expert knowledge of how it was assembled. Within minutes, the rear wheel was free and a lever was being applied to the tyre.

Molay was all the time edging towards the living-room. There was a window there, through which he meant to launch himself if the opportunity occurred.

L

Angriz went to the outer door. He spoke to the *gendarmes* waiting there.

"Three of you go to the rear of the premises. If Molay tries to leave by the window stop him, even if you have to shoot him down."

Molay ceased his covert movements towards the living-room.

Lotti had removed the tyre from the rear wheel and was feeling at the inner tube. Taking out a knife, he began to cut open the rubber. The packages came to light.

"Why, Inspector!" Molay might have been genuinely surprised. "What have you there?"

"Rather," Lotti retorted grimly, "what is it you've been hiding here?"

Molay came closer to look at the white powder Lotti had poured from a package on to the palm of his hand.

"Ah, someone has been having a joke with Molay. Putting salt in his bicycle tyres."

"Salt!" Lotti was coldly furious. "This is heroin!"

"Heroin. You—"

"Be silent! Subterfuge won't help you now. We have almost all the members of the ring in gaol already. We know who handed you this stuff. We know some of the agents who relieved you of it. We're taking you to the station to charge you."

Molay's face was flushed with rage. He hated to be spoken to in this way by men he regarded as inferior to himself. He would have given much to get his hands on Lotti for a few moments. But he knew he would be overpowered before he could really move.

The sergeant came over to him, and snapped on handcuffs.

"You'll be sorry for this! You can prove nothing

against me. Nothing! You'll look the fools you are before I've finished with you."

The two inspectors ignored his outburst. *Gendarmes* were on hand to bundle him into the car drawn right up to the door as he was brought out. Lotti and Angriz took their place side by side in the leading car, after detailing a couple of men to remain on guard at the shop.

"You see, *mon ami*, everything is falling into place perfectly. A little while ago you were asking for evidence. Now we have it. Some forty packets of it, with probably more that may yet be found on his premises. We can now establish his motive for murdering Lucille Evremont."

Angriz nodded. As Lotti had said, Molay had killed Lucille Evremont because he was sure that way he would keep secret the fact that he trafficked in drugs. But the inspector could not altogether overcome a sense of regret. This meant they were no nearer to finding the killer of Antonina Sagin and Victoroire le Bonn.

At the station, Molay was taken through into the office of Inspector Angriz. Two *gendarmes* were detailed to remain in the room.

Molay was still in a truculent, defiant mood.

"Now, charge away! Just because someone leaves a cycle at my shop with heroin hidden in it, what does that prove?"

"A court will decide that," Lotti replied. "We shall certainly prefer several charges against you regarding the heroin. But that is not our primary concern."

"Oh! Then what is, Monsieur Inspector?"

"Murder!"

Molay stared, nonplussed.

"Murder?" He was thinking of Antonina Sagin and Victoroire le Bonn. Could it be that they had unearthed something about one of those? Had he overlooked something which they had found after all these months?"

"Yes. The murder of Lucille Evremont."

Molay was some moments absorbing this. Then he began to laugh.

"Be quiet!" Lotti commanded coldly. "Murder is not a laughing matter."

"No, Inspector, murder is not funny. But your charge is."

"You will find it is very serious, indeed."

Molay was more sombre in mood now. Much as he despised the police, he was well aware of Lotti's reputation.

"You are making a very big mistake, Inspector."

"Oh, no. It was you who made the mistake when you murdered Lucille Evremont."

"I tell you I did not kill her. Why should I?"

"Why? Because you were helping to distribute heroin, and Lucille Evremont was investigating the matter. She visited your shop and discovered you were mixed up in the business. You fell to her charms, as several had done before you, and she persuaded you to talk. Or else she saw something which established your guilt. In any case, you had a very good reason to want her dead."

Molay, who had not felt particularly concerned until now, was shocked. So the girl was attached to the police. He had never given much thought to that possibility. He had been so absorbed by her beauty, he had seen her simply as a woman—as the most desirable he had ever known.

Then she had allowed him—even encouraged him—to make his advances because that was simply part of her work as an agent. It was not his size and strength, not even his masculinity, which had made her so amenable to his overtures.

He felt a sharp stab of alarm. If Lucille Evremont had been attached to the police, then someone would be made to pay the supreme penalty for her death. With a chill clarity, he saw that he was being groomed as the victim.

"We also know that you lied about your alibi. You claimed you spent the evening with Jean Gavroche. Gavroche has not corroborated that statement. In fact, he has denied that he saw you that evening. He has signed a written statement to the effect that he was at home all that evening with his wife."

"Why, the little rat! He is lying!"

"On the contrary, now that he is free of your threats and no longer has cause to fear you, he is telling the truth."

Molay was beginning to feel that walls were inexorably closing in on him. He had been a fool to trust Gavroche. He should have seen that the police would not find it hard to frighten the little runt into blabbing the truth.

"All right, all right! So the clever inspector has found out that Molay was not at home all the evening of the ninth of May. But that does not make Molay a murderer."

"Then what does it make him?" Lotti demanded.

"A gentleman."

The four men in the room stared hard at him.

"I was protecting the honour of a lady."

"You!" Angriz spoke for the first time. "You don't know the meaning of the word."

"*Gendarmes*, and especially inspectors, are not noted for their courtesy. I spent the evening with a married woman."

"Who?"

"Inspector Lotti, that is why I claimed I stayed at home. I did not wish it to be known that this lady was having an *affaire* with me."

"The name of this lady?"

"How can I tell you that?"

"You face a charge of murder. The testimony of this—this 'lady'—might save your life."

"At the expense of her honour. Molay does not wish to sink to the level of the police. Besides, her testimony will not be needed."

"Why not?"

"Because I did not kill Lucille Evremont."

Lotti was not impressed. Angriz, however, felt the doubt that had never quite left him, strengthening again. He had no illusions about Molay. He detested the man, for he was surly and savage. He knew he was a criminal and capable of downright cruelty. But there was something in Molay's attitude which he found disturbing.

It seemed the man had shown genuine surprise on being accused of murder. Of course, he might have felt so safe that he had been altogether sure he could not be accused. Nevertheless, Angriz could not persuade himself that this was so.

Lotti proceeded to make the formal charge. Molay listening with an expression of resentment and bewilderment.

"I tell you," he protested hotly in answer to it, "you are making a grave mistake."

"Your lawyers will have every chance to prove that at the right time." He nodded towards the waiting *gendarmes*. "Lock him up!"

For a few tense moments, it seemed that Molay meant to resist, but he shrugged and allowed himself to be led away.

Lotti sank back into his chair, his lean face expressing complete satisfaction. He looked at Angriz.

"Well, well! So you are still not satisfied. You still do not believe Molay killed Lucille Evremont. In heaven's name, why?"

"It is not a matter of believing. I am not so sure that the evidence against him is adequate."

"You fear I have laid the charge of murder prematurely?"

"No. But I wonder whether a court will be satisfied?"

"That is always in doubt until the jury have returned their verdict. And I can vouch for one thing."

"Yes?"

"I have taken cases into court by no means as strong as this one, and I have secured the verdict of guilty. And I will tell you something else, Inspector."

"What is that?"

"*I am absolutely certain that Molay murdered Lucille Evremont.* If he is not our man, then who is?"

Angriz had never heard anyone speak with a greater confidence.

"Yes, yes, of course. It must be Molay."

"It has to be. We have accounted for all other possibilities. There is not another man who had the motive and the opportunity. Already we have broken down

his alibi. We shall have no difficulty in showing him
to be a liar. As far as I am concerned, the case is as
good as closed. All that remains are the inevitable
formalities, and the equally inevitable end."

In his cell, Molay had opportunity to take stock of
his position. The more he thought about it, the more
anxious he became. The situation was certainly menacing. His lawyer, Albert Aldebrand, although professing great confidence in the outcome of the trial, was
obviously concerned.

"It is useless denying the heroin charge, Molay. The
police have found traces of it in several frames. They
have also gone very fully into the question of your
financial position. You have thousands of francs salted
away. What explanation are we to offer for the possession of such a large sum?"

"The shop—"

"That would not stand up for a moment. Besides,
it is bad strategy to deny what can be so readily proved
against you. And my chief concern is with the murder
charge."

Molay nodded. "I am in your hands, Monsieur
Aldebrand. What line do you propose to take?"

"There is a strategy I feel we might follow that
might well secure you an acquittal. The law regards
trafficking in drugs as a very serious matter. Very well.
The punishment is almost certain to be severe. But
you cannot refute the charge. Almost everyone implicated in the business has been arrested. Marcel
Cavanne is one of them. The police can prove that he
passed the heroin to bargees who handed it to Gavroche. Gavroche has confessed that he passed the stuff
to you."

"If I could lay my hands on that treacherous little Gavroche!" Molay uttered a string of oaths.

"Listen!" Aldebrand was young and eager to make a name for himself. He knew that, in this case, he had a rare chance to establish himself in the public mind. "We go into court openly admitting you were engaged in the drug traffic. You are sorry. But you were poor. After all, you had been apprenticed to the trade. Repairing and dealing in cycles was your only means of earning a livelihood. But business was bad—practically non-existent. Your position was parlous. It was then that Marcel Cavanne approached you with his offer. Was it surprising that you accepted it? You see, I want to create an impression. An impression of a man who is not trying to hide anything. You admit doing wrong, but you were under pressure."

Molay saw the astuteness of the idea. After all, if the murder charge was accepted by the court, he would not have to serve a prison term for dealing in drugs. It was clever to use a confession of one crime to make it appear he was innocent of another.

"But I *am* innocent of the death of Lucille Evremont."

"Yes, yes, of course." But it was obvious that Aldebrand did not believe him. "It is my duty to satisfy the court that you are."

"But you do not think you can, do you?"

"I never consider failure as a possibility. I mean to prepare the strongest case possible. It is a pity you relied on Gavroche, but that is not by any means decisive. If he is the kind of man you say he is, then it will be a very simple matter to discredit him in the eyes of the jury. I will so frighten him he will contradict himself half-a-dozen different ways within a few minutes."

In spite of these assurances, Molay was by no means satisfied. He saw the case against him as very black indeed. And he burnt with indignation. To be convicted of a crime he had not committed! To suffer the supreme penalty for a girl he had not killed! That aroused in him almost unbearable emotions. Had he had the joy of the murder, then, hard as it would be to die, at least he would be sustained by the knowledge that he had called the tune. But he had not. Yet he was to pay!

Hour by hour, day by day, the same thought went through his mind. *I am innocent. I am innocent. I am innocent.* It tormented him. It excited in him a scalding sort of anguish. He would take hold of the bars of his cell, tugging on them in his impotence.

There were moments when he felt that he was going mad. He knew the meaning of hell on earth for the first time in his life. It was self-imposed by the conviction that he was to be the victim of a monstrous injustice.

Inspector Angriz was not satisfied, either. Lotti had returned to Paris, quite certain that Molay's days were numbered.

"He's a brute," he had said to Angriz just before leaving. "A barbarian. Death is much too good for him."

Angriz had expressed no disagreement. He had reason to be grateful to Lotti. The inspector had been able to deal with the narcotics traffic which had been centred in the town. He had provided what appeared to be conclusive evidence that Molay was the one who had killed Lucille. It was Lotti who had made possible such an early arrest.

Angriz, however, was still puzzled. The murderer of Antonina Sagin and Victoroire le Bonn was still at large. He might strike again, leaving no more evidence of his identity than on previous occasions. He found it difficult to accept the facts, even though they appeared to fit so perfectly together. One fact, he felt, challenged the others.

Two murderers in Avigron! Two stranglers, at that! Yet, if the evidence was to be believed—and there seemed no reason to doubt it—there were two killers. Two men who had disposed of their victims in exactly the same way—by choking them to death. And in a small provincial town, too.

One murderer—well, that was reasonable. But everything indicated there were two. In fact, every expert who had been called in to deal with the case was sure of that. The man who had killed Sagin and le Bonn had not killed Lucille Evremont.

Angriz had to accept the argument as impeccable. A man who had strangled twice to satisfy a perversion would not strangle a third time without satisfying it again. That was not to be disputed.

Angriz chided himself for worrying further about the matter. He told himself that it was foolish to allow a feeling—intuition, he supposed it was—to make him uneasy. And, anyway, the problem was not his. The court would decide. All he had to do was to give his evidence as concisely as he could.

It was then that something happened which dispelled the inspector's doubts. He was busy in his office dealing with routine matters, when the *gendarme* on duty at the desk informed him that a young woman, Cosette Baptiste, wished to see him.

"What does she want?" he asked over the intercom.

"She says she has valuable information regarding the Molay case."

"Send her in at once."

This was it, Angriz told himself. Here was the information he had all the time feared must come up. This woman would provide the evidence to show Molay was innocent. His intuition had misled him on occasion, but not when it had been persistent as it had about Molay.

When he saw Cosette, he had no doubts about her character. Everything about her proclaimed what she was. A simple soul, aware of her plainness. No doubt, as the wide-set eyes and the full mouth proclaimed, she liked being loved. But her nondescript features and her far from impressive figure suggested she had been starved of ardent attentions from the male sex.

She seemed nervous on entering the room, her hands clearly betraying the stress and tension she was experiencing.

"Sit down, please, *Mademoiselle*." He smiled, indicating a chair facing his desk.

She complied, eyeing him uncertainly.

"Well. Why do you wish to see me?"

"It's—well, it's difficult, Inspector."

"Take your time. I've all day." That was by no means true, but he had to win her confidence. This girl's information, he felt sure, might prevent a grave miscarriage of justice.

"Pierre Molay? He—he won't be free for a long time, will he?"

"He might never be free again. But why do you ask?"

Cosette was twisting her fingers and untwisting them repeatedly. 'If he got free he might—well, he might kill me—if he knew I'd told."

Angriz waited. This was certainly not the kind of thing he had expected.

"You need not be afraid of him. Molay will never be able to hurt you."

"Never? You're sure of that, Inspector?"

"I promise you—never."

She was silent for some moments, then she said: "Lucille Evremont—she—she was killed in the Forêt d'Antoinette, wasn't she?"

"Yes. The evidence indicates she was murdered some two hundred yards from the river."

"On the evening of May ninth?"

"That's right."

"About what time?"

"According to the medical evidence, some time between seven and half-past nine."

"Say a quarter-past eight?"

"It might well have been. When a body has been immersed in water for several hours, it's not easy to determine exactly just when the murder took place."

There was a smile on Cosette's face now. It was a smile of no little satisfaction.

"I now know for certain who killed Lucille Evremont, Inspector."

"Who?"

"It was Pierre Molay."

Angriz was surprised. He had been so sure the girl had come forward to say it was *not* Molay.

"You're sure of this?"

"Oh, I'm sure all right."

"You know, of course, that you are making a very serious statement. How can you be so sure?"

"Because I followed him to the edge of the Forêt d'Antoinette on May the ninth."

Angriz was leaning over the desk. "You followed him? Why?"

"Because I knew he was going to meet that Lucille Evremont."

"You knew? How could you know?"

"Oh, I knew all right." The smile of satisfaction had been replaced by a rising indignation. "You see, Pierre was my man. He was my lover. Oh, and Pierre could love. He is so strong, so full of vigour—"

"Yes, yes, I am sure. Pierre Molay was your lover, and I'm sure he was all you say. But how does this concern Lucille Evremont."

"How? Because he made love to her."

"You seem sure of that."

"Oh, I am sure. I went into his shop. She was in the back with him. He came out, and his face betrayed what he had been doing with the Evremont woman. Besides, she came to the door of the living-room and she was putting her skirt straight. And her hair, it was all untidy."

Angriz was beginning to get the picture into perspective.

The girl had seen Lucille Evremont go to Molay's premises. When Lucille had not reappeared after quite some time, jealousy had excited suspicion in Cosette's breast, and she had gone into the shop. No doubt, disturbing Molay in his love-making. And there could be no doubt, too, about Molay's reactions. He would be furious.

"I take it Molay ordered you to leave?"

"He did more than that. He almost threw me out. And for her!"

"I would try not to feel too badly about her. She is dead. And she was very beautiful."

"But she stole my man!"

Angriz wondered. Molay had never been her man in the way Cosette had imagined. But she had been unable to see that. In any case, it was a matter of no importance now.

"After he had sent you away, *Mademoiselle*, what did you do?"

"I waited where I couldn't be seen from the shop. I wanted to see the woman go away."

"And you did?"

"Yes. She did not stay more than a few minutes, not after I'd been there. But I felt sure she would come back."

"Ah, now I see. You spied on the premises."

"I did. But she did not come back. Instead, he went out."

"What time?"

"I cannot be sure to the minute. I have no watch. But it was some time after half-past seven, I would say. He didn't see me. He just went to the dirt path that leads to the track that skirts the Forêt d'Antoinette."

"Just?"

"I mean straight. He didn't look to one side or the other. But when he got down the path, he acted strangely."

"In what way?"

"He kept looking back."

"Did he see you?"

"See me? No. I didn't intend him to. It wasn't hard to keep out of his sight. The path is narrow and winding."

Angriz had no doubts now.

"How far did you follow him?"

"To the track that runs at the side of the forest. Then I knew he was expecting to meet someone."

"Did you see him meet Lucille Evremont?"

Cosette shook her head. "Oh, no! I saw him to the road on the edge of the forest, and I knew then what he was up to. But I dare not be seen. He would have killed me."

"So you came back home?"

"Yes, Inspector."

Angriz felt as if a shadow had been dispelled from his mind. They had in Cosette a virtual witness to the crime. Her evidence would be conclusive. She was too simple and artless to make up her story. It had the unmistakable ring of truth.

"Tell me, what has made you come to us now?"

"He betrayed me! He said I was his girl. But he lied! Lied!"

Angriz leaned back in his chair. Cosette had been scorned. Feeling safe from Molay, she was intent on revenge. It was as simple—and sordid—as that!

"You will make a statement and sign it?"

"Of course. That is why I came here."

"You will have to appear in court. You know that?"

"Oh, yes! I don't mind. I don't mind at all."

So the girl had the vanity to court publicity. She was set on having her moment of dubious glory. Defending Counsel would make her look a far from admirable figure. Still, she would be a key—perhaps *the* key witness. Her picture would appear in all the papers, and she would be pointed out as a girl who had gained a lover.

It was an hour later that Cosette Baptiste left the station. Behind her she left several copies of her signed statement. As Inspector Angriz read through it he realised that he had in his hands Pierre Molay's death warrant.

He put through a telephone call to Inspector Lotti, in Paris.

"So, *mon ami*, we have given the key its final twist. The blade is already poised above Molay's head. With a witness like that his last hope of escape has gone. He is as good as dead."

Angriz, although he did not quite share Lotti's jubilation, was easy in his mind. It was a great relief to him to be free of all doubt. A man who made no claim to subtlety and cunning, he saw things in graphic and realistic terms. Executions horrified him. And the thought of unjustly depriving a man of his life had worried him greatly.

"France will be a little healthier when he has gone," Lotti was saying over the 'phone. "Molay is evil. He does not rank as human. No one will regret his death —least of all myself!"

Everything happened exactly as Inspector Lotti had predicted. The case captured the attention of all France, and most of the countries of Europe. It had everything. A beautiful victim, who had been dedicated to stamping out the drug traffic and bringing to justice every man engaged in it.

The accused was thoroughly male, and built on grand proportions. Counsel on both sides were grimly determined and no quarter was asked or given.

M

Throughout, Molay reiterated his innocence. But it was hopeless from the start. His own admissions prejudiced the court, and the country, against him. He had not hesitated to engage in distributing heroin, and over several months in considerable quantities. He was a proven liar, having claimed to have spent the critical evening with Gavroche when Gavroche testified, however nervously, that he, himself, had been at home with his wife. And Gavroche's wife, a sour and resentful witness, corroborated her husband's testimony. He had, indeed, spent the whole of the evening of May ninth with her.

Even without Cosette's evidence, the position looked black for Molay. But her account of what happened on the day and evening Lucille Evremont lost her life, spelt *fini*. It was true that the woman was too naive to conceal her satisfaction at being the centre of national attention. Nor could she hide her jealousy of Lucille. Nevertheless, her story was so obviously true, and all defence Counsel's efforts to shake her proved unavailing. Her very simplicity proved her protection against his repeated scathing attacks on her moral character.

There were many dramatic moments during the trial, but the most sensational came immediately after the court had made its findings known.

Even as the presiding judge pronounced the death penalty, Pierre Molay began to pound upon the woodwork of the dock with clenched hands, and to shout:

"I am innocent! Innocent! I tell you I did not kill Lucille Evremont!"

CHAPTER XVI

THE OUTBURST had an electrifying effect on everyone who witnessed it. There was something almost awesome in the sight of this Titan so desperately roaring that he was guiltless of the crime for which he had been sentenced to death.

Pandemonium followed. Some eight *gendarmes* struggled to get him away. For several seconds, he resisted their combined efforts to prise loose his hands from the front of the dock. And all the time he was screaming:

"Fools! Fools! I tell you I did not kill the woman Evremont. I did not even see her that night. I am innocent—innocent, I tell you!"

It was a relief when he had at last been dragged out of sight to the cells below the court, and his protests could be heard no longer.

One man who remained unaffected by the commotion was Inspector Lotti. He sought out Inspector Angriz to bid him *au revoir*, knowing he intended to return to Avigron as soon as the case was closed.

"There will almost certainly be an appeal. But it will come to nothing. Aldebrand can but delay the inevitable end."

"Yes, of course. Thank you for your invaluable help, Inspector." Angriz embraced Lotti. He was, although he did not say so, feeling unusually emotional. Molay's outburst had disturbed him deeply. But, knowing how Lotti felt about the matter, he said nothing.

Nevertheless, there had been something in Molay's

manner which had served to bring flooding back all
the doubts Angriz had felt sure he had discarded for
good. No man could act as he had acted unless under
the spur of a compelling emotion. Molay had protested
his innocence because he *was* innocent. Angriz was
convinced of that. In spite of all the evidence, in spite
of the verdict returned against him, Molay had not
killed Lucille Evremont.

The conviction made him thoroughly unhappy. He
wanted to believe Molay guilty. He disliked Molay
intensely. The man *was* a monster—a barbarian. He
deserved no sympathy. He was entitled to no consideration. Nevertheless, it was wrong for him to die
for a murder he had not committed.

Besides, if Angriz was right, then he had two very
serious problems still to solve. He was in charge of a
town where there were two unsolved killings. The
near complacency he had felt during the last few
weeks, had quite vanished. With two murderers at
large, there could be others who would lose their lives.

Yet what could he do? Officially, the case was closed.
With what did he challenge the evidence? He had
nothing at all to go on except his feelings. He had
nothing concrete with which to support his certainty.
He was helpless.

He viewed the future with no little foreboding.
With dread he noted the inexorable approach of the
day of execution on his office calendar. He also felt
there would be other murders in due course which
he would be powerless to prevent.

As expected, an appeal was made and dismissed.
All that now stood between Molay and death was the
clemency of the President. No one believed that it
would be exercised. On what grounds could the head

of the State interfere with the normal course of justice?
There was not a single mitigating circumstance to help
him. No one would say a word in his favour.

It was the day before the date fixed for the execution that Angriz received the unexpected request.
Pierre Molay wished to see him.

Angriz felt a great reluctance to comply with it. But
he knew he had no choice. Molay might wish to give
him information which would be of value. It did not
seem a likely explanation, for Molay had lost no opportunity to make it clear how much he hated the police.
Nevertheless, the request had been prompted by something. Nothing could be lost by finding out what it
was.

Feeling unusually tense, Angriz made the journey
to Paris. He was conducted on arrival at the prison to
the condemned cell.

"You are the only one he has asked to see," said the
governor. "I must say I thought it a strange request—
the wish to see one of the men responsible for him
being where he is. If you think he might attack you,
I—"

"I'm sure he will not. I don't suppose I'll be allowed
to see him alone?"

"No. Not even you, Inspector. He is guarded
twenty-four hours a day by three men."

Angriz was relieved on seeing Molay. Although he
must have been under great strain, he was refusing to
break down. He looked pale and drawn, and Angriz
thought he was thinner. But it was soon obvious that
his manner had not changed.

"So you decided to come, Inspector!"

"Obviously." Angriz, as always, found his sympathy
evaporating the moment he was in the man's presence.

He was still surly and hostile. "Why do you wish to see me?"

"To tell you I am innocent."

This was what he had feared.

"The court did not say so. Nor has the appeal court. Even the President—"

"I know, I know! But what does he know about the matter?"

"Listen, Molay. You asked me to come here. I have made the journey from Avigron hoping you had something to tell me that you had not yet told to anyone. Merely to say that you did not kill Lucille Evremont—"

"But I did not kill her. Don't you see? Don't you understand? That is what is so terrible about it. I am to die for a crime I did not commit."

"Even if you are speaking the truth, what do you expect me to do about it?"

"But you do not believe me. That's it, isn't it. Molay has been discarded as worthless. So, worthless, he is to die for something he did not do. Is that right?"

"Were it so, it would not be right. But the evidence—"

Molay lifted clenched hands in a despairing gesture.

"The evidence! Bah! You know it was not enough. I saw it in your face at the trial. Oh, the other inspector was satisfied, but not you. I tell you, I set out to meet Lucille Evremont, but she was not at the rendezvous. Someone met her before I did. It was that someone who killed her. Not Molay! Oh, no, Inspector, I did not kill her."

Angriz was sure that Molay was telling the truth. Still, he could not see that he could do anything to save Molay from the knife. There was no new positive evidence that would justify a stay of execution.

"Listen, listen! If I had killed her, I would die happily—at least, without complaining. But the guilty man is free. He is free! Don't you understand?"

Angriz understood only too well. It was a thought which had given him some very unhappy moments. He knew it was one that would cause him a great deal of uncertainty in the future. Had he not been helpless. . . .

"It doesn't matter whether I believe you're innocent, or whether I think you're guilty. There is nothing I can do. There is nothing anyone can do."

"Fool! Fool!" The veins were standing out on Molay's forehead. "Cannot you see—"

"It is pointless me staying longer merely to suffer your abuse." Angriz moved towards the door.

"No, no!" Molay's voice was so very earnest, Angriz paused. "I did not kill Lucille Evremont. I must make you believe that. I cannot die for a crime I did not commit. I cannot."

"I'm sorry, Molay. You cannot convince me."

"But I can! I can! I killed Antonina Sagin! I killed Victoroire le Bonn!"

Angriz had already turned. "*You?*"

"I have said so. But I did not kill Lucille Evremont."

Angriz felt a thrill of triumph. He knew the truth now. Molay was responsible for the two most terrible murders.

"Are you willing to sign a confession that you killed Antonina Sagin and Victoroire le Bonn?"

"If I am not to be executed for a crime of which I am innocent."

Angriz was thoughtful for some moments.

"Do you know who *did* kill Lucille?"

"No. I meant to. Oh, yes, I meant to all right. The way I had killed the others. But someone beat me to it."

"Have you no idea who it was?"

"Oh, yes. She had been active against the narcotics ring. Why shouldn't one of them have killed her?"

"Who?"

"Marcel Cavanne. He would not hesitate to destroy anyone who threatened the organisation. Supposing he found out about Lucille Evremont and followed her to Avigron?"

Angriz was thinking hard. The pieces in the jig-saw were beginning to fall into place now. Molay might be wrong about Cavanne, but some other member of the organisation might well have accounted for poor Lucille.

"This is for people far higher than I, Molay. But I will contact the authorities and explain to them the situation. You must know, of course, that this can only delay your end."

"Yes. I am not a fool. But at least I shall die for the things I did, and not—"

"Very well."

Angriz hurried away.

His first contact was Inspector Lotti. Lotti, initially, was furious with the turn of events. Eventually, however, he saw that he had no choice but to report to the head of the Sûreté.

The execution was postponed, causing a sensation throughout France. With Lotti, he visited Marcel Cavanne in prison.

He greeted them with a chill hostility.

"I do not answer questions that will incriminate either myself or my comrades."

"Not even to say whether or not you murdered Lucille Evremont?"

"Murdered her?" The eyes glittered fiercely. "It was Molay—"

"Oh, no!" Lotti cut in.

"But—"

"Molay did not murder Lucille Evremont. Perhaps you did?"

"I? Marcel Cavanne? I loved her. With all my heart I loved her."

"But she deceived you."

"Ah, yes, she deceived me."

"Then how can we be sure you did not kill her for revenge?"

"How? You can be sure, Inspector, because I still love her. No matter what Lucille did to me, I should love her. That I cannot help. My head tells my heart that it is foolish, but my heart cannot hear.

"Lucille was beautiful. The most beautiful woman I have ever met. Oh, her face! Ravishing! And her figure! Were there ever such breasts? To see them— touch them! What delight. What madness! And was there ever a woman who could love like her? With such understanding? Such abandonment? Ah, I never knew there could be such rapture—such ecstasy! I always thought my Rebecca knew all the arts of love."

"Rebecca is your wife?"

"Of course—my wife. I was so happy with her until Lucille loved me. But then I saw that Rebecca was like a big and very amiable cow. Maternal, you know. For a long time, I was content with her. Then I realised how much I had missed."

A few minutes later, they left Cavanne.

"No, he didn't kill Lucille," said Lotti. "That much is obvious. The problem is, who did?"

"Perhaps we shall find the answer to that back in Avigron. I think it more than likely that we shall. At the Hôtel Majestique."

"Would you like me to return there with you?"

"If you can spare the time, Inspector, I should greatly appreciate your assistance."

"I'd like to. I'd hate to leave the case where it is, but I have no wish to intrude."

It was not until the next day that the two inspectors visited the Hôtel Majestique. Lotti was the first to reach the semi-circular desk.

"We'd like to see your register for the period covering the first two weeks of May."

Without a word, the receptionist flicked back the leaves. He turned it round to face them and pointed to the date at the top of the page.

"You remember Mademoiselle Lucille Evremont?" Lotti asked, his index finger moving down the names.

"Do I look the kind of idiot who would forget her?"

"Answer my questions. Don't try to be clever. This is a most serious matter."

The clerk did not reply. But it was obvious he was not abashed.

"Was there any man staying here when Mademoiselle Evremont was a guest who was a stranger to you?"

"I don't remember one."

"Think! A man who was big."

The clerk shook his head. "Not a man. A woman."

"A woman?"

"A big woman."

"What name did she register under?" Angriz asked.

"That one." The clerk pointed. "Costair—Madame Costair."

"Yes. I remember her well. I was struck by her great physical strength. She was big—very big for a woman. But feminine for all that."

"It seems you have a theory, *mon ami*. What is it?"

"I would be more sure if the name of this woman had not been Costair." Angriz turned to the clerk. "Where did Madame Costair come from?"

"She did not say."

"When did she leave."

The clerk consulted another ledger. "On the eleventh of May."

"Two days after the murder." Lotti pursed his lips. "Did she say where she was going?"

"No. I was off duty when she decided to leave. My relief ordered her a taxi to take her to the station. That's all I can tell you."

"I think that is all we need to know. *Merci*."

They were back in Angriz' office when he said:

"I suppose it was a natural mistake to make, centring all our thoughts on a man as a murderer. After all, what more reasonable? Who would think of a woman killing Lucille Evremont, and least of all by strangulation? Such an idea never occurred to me."

Lotti nodded. "Nor me. I was confident it must be a man engaged in the distribution of heroin. After all, she was risking being murdered all the time, and she knew it. Naturally, I concluded that someone had realised what she was up to and had decided to despatch her. Besides, who would think of a woman strong enough to carry the girl so far from the point of killing to the river?"

"One woman was capable of such a feat—and she proved it."

"Your Madame Costair?"

"Exactly."

"And if you are right about her, we shall find her in Perpignan."

"Tomorrow?"

"Yes, tomorrow. But I think we ought to go there as quickly as we can. How about travelling tonight. Molay's reprieve might have aroused her suspicions."

The two inspectors were in the little fortified town of Perpignan early the following morning.

The local police supplied them with the address they needed, and also provided a couple of *gendarmes* to go along with them.

The house proved to be neat and very tidy, the whitewashed walls looking bright in the climbing sun.

It was the woman they sought who opened the door to them.

"Madame Costair?" Inspector Lotti bowed. "Or should I say Madame Cavanne?"

"The police?" She showed little surprise. "You wish to see me?"

"Please."

"Then come in." She led the way to the living-room.

Angriz was struck by her motherly air. He was also alive to the great weight of sadness that seemed to press down on her huge shoulders. She looked much older than when he had last seen her. Shadows had gathered about her eyes.

"Can I get you a glass of wine, gentlemen?"

"It's too early for me, thank you," said Angriz.

"And me. Thanks all the same."

"Then perhaps you'll sit down?"

The two *gendarmes* had stayed outside on guard. The inspectors sank down into easy chairs. Everything in the room suggested comfort.

"You *are* the wife of Marcel Cavanne, aren't you?" asked Lotti.

"That's right."

"And you registered at the Hôtel Majestique in—"

"As Madame Costair. Yes, Inspector."

"Why?"

"Obviously to hide my identity."

"Why should you wish to do that?"

"You know the answer to that one, don't you?"

Lotti nodded.

"In fact, you're here because you know that I killed Lucille Evremont."

"We felt reasonably sure you had. Why did you do it? Because Lucille was working to expose your husband, and have him brought to justice as a distributor of drugs?"

"Oh, no! I didn't realise what she was until—until after she was dead. She came to this town, pretending to be on a long holiday. I gave her little thought—at first. In fact, I was hardly conscious of her until I became aware of the truth."

"The truth?"

"That she was taking Marcel away from me." She spread her large hands. She eased her great frame to a more comfortable position in the chair. "Oh, there had been other women before her. Women younger than I, and far better looking. But they had only been birds of passage. He had spent a few nights with them, and that was invariably the end. Always he would

come back to me, and usually he was very contrite,
although I told him there was no reason to be. I understood his needs, you see. And I thought he understood
mine—until the truth opened up before me like some
great black hole."

"Your husband was really in love with Lucille?"

"Yes. I would not have cared had he made love to
her a few times and then forgotten her. But no! This
was a quite different *affaire*. He wanted her, and only
her."

"I can readily understand that. Lucille had her own
particular kind of magic."

"Oh, she was very, very beautiful. In comparison, I
was what Marcel described me—a big and amiable
cow."

Angriz remembered. Those were the very words he
had used when describing his wife to them.

"But Marcel was my husband. He was more. He was
also my child. You see, we had no children. I missed
them a great deal. But Marcel loved to be my child.
He would lie in my arms while I soothed him. He was
a brave man, my Marcel. Yet he was also a little boy.
He liked to feel my arms around him. He used to say
they made him feel safe. Although the things he was
afraid of were not the police. They were things inside
him, connected with the war, if you understand?"

Angriz nodded. "I think we do."

"So you see, *Messieurs*, Marcel was my everything
—my life. I could lend him a little while—for a night
or two now and then—but I could not lose him. And
it was too late when I saw what had happened. He
didn't want me any more. Not at all. There was only
one woman for him, he said. This Lucille Evremont."

There was an elongated silence. Then the large

hands were spread again, the gesture indicating an unwilling resignation.

"There was only one thing I could do. I had to kill her. I could not bear her to have my Marcel. Oh, I knew I had lost him. But I still hoped that, if he knew Lucille was for ever beyond his reach, he might come back to me again. But if not, she still had to die. After all, it was only just."

"Just?" Lotti leaned forward to catch the quietly spoken words.

"Yes, Inspector. She had already killed me."

"What a pity you didn't know the facts. You see, Lucille Evremont did not love your husband. She hated him. Hated him because he was engaged in a traffic which had destroyed her sister."

Madame Cavanne sighed heavily. "Ah, yes, I realised that later. But it makes no difference. Marcel still loved her. She had turned his heart away from me."

She pushed herself out of her chair.

"I must go with you, Inspector Angriz?"

"I'm afraid so."

"I suppose I can get one or two things—a few toilet requisites?"

She went from the room to the rear of the house.

"What an unholy business! What tragedy! Who would be a policeman at such a time. She looks really pathetic."

Lotti nodded. "So did Lucille when I saw her in the mortuary."

Angriz did not pursue the conversation further. He lit the cigarette the Sûreté man declined. They waited. They became aware of a deep silence which had suddenly taken possession of the house. They exchanged a significant glance. Lotti hurried through to the back, Angriz on his heels.

Madame Cavanne lay on her bed. She might have been asleep, she looked so peaceful.

"*Mon Dieu!*" Lotti made a brief examination. "She's slipped through our fingers. But I alone am to blame for that, I should never have allowed her out of my sight."

He sniffed at the glass phial near the hand of the dead woman. There was an unmistakable smell of bitter almonds.

"She has taken cyanide, *mon ami*."

Angriz crossed himself before replying.

"Evidently she expected us to catch up with her, and had prepared for our arrival."

"No. I think not. Cyanide cannot be obtained so easily these days. During the war, however, such phials were issued to top men in the Resistance for use in moments of extremity. Marcel Cavanne was one of them. Confronted with just such a situation, *Madame* remembered where it was kept. Anticipating the sentence of the court, she decided to carry it out in her own way—"

Lotti did not complete his exposition, but turned again to the bed. Slowly, he drew up the sheet until it covered the serene face of Madame Cavanne.

FIN